Bev —

I hope you enjoy the book.

Best wishes!

Kathryn Jesson
Nov: 2010

# THE DESIRES OF OPULENCE

by
KATHRYN JESSON

iUniverse, Inc.
New York  Bloomington

# THE DESIRES OF OPULENCE

*Copyright © 2010 by Kathryn Jesson*

*All rights reserved. No part of this book may be used or reproduced by any means, graphic, electronic, or mechanical, including photocopying, recording, taping or by any information storage retrieval system without the written permission of the publisher except in the case of brief quotations embodied in critical articles and reviews.*

*iUniverse books may be ordered through booksellers or by contacting:*
*iUniverse*
*1663 Liberty Drive*
*Bloomington, IN 47403*
*www.iuniverse.com*
*1-800-Authors (1-800-288-4677)*

*Because of the dynamic nature of the Internet, any Web addresses or links contained in this book may have changed since publication and may no longer be valid. This is a work of fiction. All of the characters, names, incidents, organizations, and dialogue in this novel are either the products of the author's imagination or are used fictitiously..*

*ISBN: 978-1-4502-2383-6 (pbk)*
*ISBN: 978-1-4502-2384-3 (ebk)*

*Printed in the United States of America*

*iUniverse rev. date: 4/23/10*

*To my husband, Mike.*
*Thank you for your love, friendship and encouragement.*

# *Acknowledgements*

Thank you to my editor, Dustin Dinoff, for your enthusiasm and candor; to Anya Wassenberg and Sandra LeFaucheur for sharing your writing experiences and knowledge with me. My sincere appreciation to Constable Patricia Thiessen of the Niagara Police Service's Central Fraud Unit, and from Peel Regional Police, Detective Frank Kavcic of the Forensic Identification Bureau and Sergeant Mark Stafford of the Marine Unit.

I wish to extend a special thank you to Peel Regional Police Sergeant Brian Wintermute for your time and expertise while attempting to teach a civilian the ins and outs of criminal fraud.

# Prologue

"Damn weather people," Margaret Ross mumbled as she flipped on the windshield wipers. "Like so many other times, they didn't call this one right."

Expecting precipitation in the form of wet snow for later that afternoon, Margaret was perturbed to see large snowflakes beginning to fall twenty minutes into her mid-morning drive.

The Niagara Peninsula had experienced a long, harsh winter and now, late in March, it wasn't giving up easily. Margaret was on her way home to Niagara-on-the-Lake after spending the weekend in Smithville visiting friends. Reaching the crest of a steep incline, Margaret was alarmed to see the roadway ahead completely covered in thick snow and two cars sideways in the ditch. She instinctively applied the brakes as her Cadillac descended the hill, and within seconds the car began to fishtail. *Steer in the direction of the skid*, Margaret told herself, but quickly realized she was unable to control the vehicle.

"Dear God!" she gasped. Panic-stricken, she gripped the steering wheel and braced herself. She was disoriented; everything was spinning around her. When the vehicle finally came to a stop, it was positioned across one lane of traffic directly in the path of an oncoming cube van. There was no time for Margaret to react. She turned her head to see the bumper, grill and headlights coming straight at her. The collision was violent as the van struck the driver's side door of the Cadillac, crushing it into the driver's compartment and shattering the window. Although Margaret was wearing a seatbelt, and the side air bags deployed, the extreme force of the impact threw her into the wreckage. Searing pain ripped through her torso and she screamed in agony. Her head slammed into the jagged metal framework of the door, then everything faded to black.

## Chapter One

"The building can't be renovated for that price, Dan! It's not up to fire code, the plumbing and hot water heating system will have to be replaced, and the restorative work on the exterior is a major undertaking. What the new owners want to spend on this warehouse won't cover two-thirds of the construction costs."

Dan Neufeld studied his employee and friend, Katelyn Ross, as she rose from her desk chair and walked over to the office window. She was strikingly beautiful, her Irish descent evident by her auburn hair, green eyes and creamy complexion. This morning she was impeccably dressed in a beige pencil skirt and matching suit jacket, a silk blouse in a terracotta shade that enhanced her hair colour, and beige pumps that showed off her slender legs.

Running his hands through his wavy, black hair, Dan sighed. Katelyn's frustration was certainly understandable. The project involved the conversion of a 1920's warehouse into ten luxury condominiums. The property owners' expectations were high, but their funding was tight. Dan surmised that at some point the issue of safety and adhering to building codes would come into play, and he was prepared to walk away from the project should there be any suggestion by the owners of compromising either in order to cut costs. Jeopardizing the reputation of his architectural firm wasn't an option.

The buzz of Katelyn's intercom interrupted his thoughts. She returned to her desk and pressed the flashing button.

"Yes, Seema?"

"There's an urgent call for you on line one," Dan's assistant replied.

"Thanks."

Dan rose from the chair to leave. "I'll give you some privacy. We can continue our discussion later."

Returning to his office, Dan pulled out the warehouse blueprints and began to examine them. Minutes later, he heard a tapping on his door, and looked up from his drawing table. "Come in, Kate. I've been looking over the plans and—" His voice trailed off at the site of her red-rimmed eyes. It appeared as though she had been crying. He asked, warily. "Kate? Are you all right?"

She slowly crossed the room, sat down in a chair situated near his desk, and looked at him blankly.

*The phone call!* "Something has happened. What is it, Kate?"

She stammered, "That, uh, that call was from the Niagara Police. My mother was in a car accident." Katelyn's bottom lip quivered as she tried to form the words. "She's, um, she's dead."

"Christ!" Dan exclaimed, springing from his stool and striding over to where she was sitting. "I'm so sorry." He sat down in the chair next to hers and gently took her small, trembling hands in his. "What can I do? How can I help?"

Katelyn looked into his intense blue eyes. "Just being here for me is enough." She shook her head. "I can't believe I'm going through this again so soon. I'm just coming to terms with Daddy's death two years ago and now—" Tears filled her eyes and quickly trailed down her flushed cheeks.

Dan clearly recalled the day when Katelyn received the news that her father had been rushed to the hospital after collapsing at home. He had suffered a heart attack and was in critical condition. By the time Katelyn's plane landed in Toronto after the four and a half hour flight from Vancouver, her father had suffered a second coronary and couldn't be revived.

Searching for words of comfort, Dan reached for the box of tissues on his desk and gently placed it in Katelyn's lap. "Life sure has a way of blindsiding us. You know that all of us here at the office will support you any way we can."

Katelyn nodded as she dabbed her eyes with a tissue. "Everyone at Neufeld, Ramcharan are like my family. I don't know what I would do without them."

Dan's heart ached to see her looking so wounded and vulnerable. He put his arm around her and she rested her head on his chest. He noticed that her hair smelled of lilac. After a few moments, he asked, "Have you made flight arrangements?"

"My travel agent is working on it right now," Katelyn replied, sniffling.

"When the time comes, I'll drive you to the airport," he stated. She began to protest, but he interrupted her. "No arguments, Kate. It's no trouble."

She lifted her head from his chest and looked up at him, smiling weakly. "You're a dear friend. Thank you."

As word of Katelyn's tragic loss quickly spread around the firm, her co-workers warmly reached out with hugs and words of comfort.

The travel agent was able to book Katelyn on the first flight out the following morning. When Dan arrived at her condominium, she appeared tired and pensive. Their conversation was minimal, mostly reassurances from him that if she needed anything, all she had to do was pick up the telephone. He stayed with her until she was ready to pass through security. He hugged her tightly. "Take all the time you need, Kate. Keep in touch."

****

As the airport limousine driver retrieved her luggage from the trunk, Katelyn stood on the snow-covered sidewalk in front of her parents' Victorian home and scanned its exterior. Although completely renovated inside, externally the house still retained the look of the late 1800's, with white clapboard siding, small-paned windows and black wooden shutters. She was relieved to see the walkway cleared of snow, probably shovelled by the same neighbour who fed her mother's cat whenever she was out of town. Katelyn thanked the driver for carrying her bags to the front door and tipped him generously.

Feeling a heaviness in her chest, Katelyn unlocked the door, took a deep breath, and stepped inside the tiny foyer. She immediately recognized the sweet aroma of rose petals, one of her mother's favourite scents. The interior of the home was simply elegant, and as always, spotlessly clean. "A place for everything and everything in its place," Margaret Ross would always say, a technique Katelyn hadn't yet been able to master.

Ashton appeared from the living room and greeted her with a long, drawn out meow.

"Ash, such a handsome boy. How are you?" cooed Katelyn as she bent down to stroke his silky soft, smoky gray fur. Purring, the cat arched his back and entwined himself around her leg. "I'll bet you're hungry. I could sure use a cup of tea right about now."

After removing her boots and hanging her full length suede coat in the closet, Katelyn made her way to the kitchen, the cat following closely behind. He waited patiently and watched her every move as she plugged in the electric kettle and retrieved a box of cat treats from the pantry. Leaving him to eat, Katelyn returned to the foyer and carried her suitcases down the hall to the master bedroom. The room was furnished with a large cherry wood four-poster bed adorned with a handmade quilt in various fabrics of plums and pinks. An antique curio cabinet displaying a collection of dainty china dolls, and a burgundy, velvet settee sat in one corner of the room. Pictures of Katelyn's great-grandparents, appearing very stoic, hung in wooden oval frames on one dusty rose wall.

Katelyn found a pair of crocheted slippers to warm up her feet, and before making her way back to the kitchen, peered inside the den, once many years ago her bedroom. Here her mother sat and watched her favourite television programs while quilting blankets, knitting sweaters or creating any number of craft projects she had taken up over the years. Katelyn's eyes were drawn to the circular table in the corner of the room where a black leather Fendi wallet lay in a box lined with pink tissue paper. Next to it was a birthday card with the words *To A Dear Daughter On Her Birthday*, and a country cottage printed on the front. The inside of the card was signed, '*All my love, Mom*'.

Suddenly overcome, Katelyn collapsed into a chair, her sobs drowning out the whistling kettle.

****

Her body aching for rest, Katelyn snuggled down into the soft cotton sheets, the faint rose scent of her mother's body lotion filling her nostrils. She recalled the nights as a little girl when she would run into this room, frightened by a nightmare or thunderstorm, and crawl into the big bed between her parents. Her mother would pull her close and kiss her on the cheek. Within moments, she would drift off to sleep to the wonderful sensation of fingers gently combing through her silky hair, her fears forgotten.

This night there was no one to comfort her, no one to hold her in their arms and tell her everything would be all right. Katelyn closed her eyes, hoping for sleep, but her mind repeatedly played out details of the telephone call from the Niagara Police officer.

"Ms. Ross, this is Sergeant Jarrod Armstrong of the Niagara Regional Police. Are you a relative of Margaret Anne Ross?"

Instantly, a feeling of dread had welled up inside her as she responded, "Yes, Margaret Anne Ross is my mother."

"Ma'am, I regret to inform you that at 10:35 this morning your mother was involved in a fatal automobile accident." The officer's tone was sympathetic, his words carefully chosen, as he described the accident scene. "The injuries were extensive—" Katelyn heard and understood every word the gentleman was saying. What she was trying so hard to grasp was that he was talking about her mother. "—her purse and its contents, car keys and overnight bag are here at the division. You are also required to attend the impound facility to remove the remaining items from the vehicle. I recommend you have a family member or friend accompany you there."

Even though it was midnight, her body clock was three hours behind on Pacific Standard Time. Surrendering to the fact that sleep wasn't coming anytime soon, Katelyn got up, leaving Ashton the bed all to himself.

****

Feeling sleep deprived and extremely apprehensive, Katelyn took comfort in knowing her best friend, Cheryl Miller, was accompanying her to the funeral home. She had known Cheryl since ninth grade, experiencing all the teenage triumphs and tribulations together: braces, acne, boys, break-ups. Cheryl was the outgoing and fun-loving half of the duo. Any trouble the two had managed to get into was usually her idea. Katelyn, on the other hand, was the serious and responsible one. The two had complemented each other back then and were pretty much inseparable.

"Dear lord, girlfriend," said Cheryl as she stepped through the doorway of the Ross home and hugged Katelyn tightly. "I'd prefer not to see you under these circumstances."

"I really appreciate your help, Cher. I can't imagine going through this by myself."

Pulling away, Cheryl laid her hands on Katelyn's shoulders and fought back the tears. "Hey, we're best buddies! If the roles were reversed, you'd be by my side in a heartbeat. Right?"

"Right," Katelyn replied.

The young women cried and hugged each other again until Cheryl broke the embrace. "Well, we'd better get going. We have a busy day ahead and standing here blubbering on each other's shoulders isn't going to help!"

Arriving at the funeral home, Katelyn stood in the entrance and watched the director walk toward her. It sickened her to think that now, tragically, both her parents were gone. *I shouldn't be here. How does a person make sense of this?* Her mother hadn't discussed her burial wishes with Katelyn; no one had expected Margaret Ross to die at fifty-nine years of age. With assistance from Cheryl and the funeral director, Katelyn made the necessary decisions she felt her mother would approve of. The director gently and compassionately recommended a closed casket for the visitation, which Katelyn agreed to. A short visitation would take place one hour before the service at the beautiful and historic St. Mark's Church. Katelyn would meet with the minister, organist and soloist to discuss her mother's favourite bible passages and hymns. Margaret Ross would be buried next to her husband in the church cemetery.

****

Sergeant Jarrod Armstrong hated this part of his job. He had been a police officer for nearly fifteen years and seeing sorrow the likes of which Katelyn Ross was experiencing over and over again in his career touched him deeply every single time.

Escorting the woman and her friend to an interview room, he carefully reiterated some of the details of the accident at her request. "Miss Ross, according to the initial report from officers of the Major Collision Bureau who reconstructed the accident scene, it appears your mother didn't suffer," he added. "When the paramedics arrived on scene minutes after the collision and examined her, all vital signs were absent, meaning she didn't have a heartbeat or pulse."

Katelyn nodded that she understood. "The man who was driving the truck, how is he doing?"

"He'll be in the hospital a few days recovering from various fractures," replied Armstrong, impressed by Katelyn's compassion.

He handed her an inventory sheet to sign. It listed a grey overnight bag, a black leather purse, its contents, and a set of keys on an *I Love Crafts* keychain. He gave Katelyn his business card, knowing from experience that family members had follow-up questions in the days and weeks following a tragedy. The officer strongly emphasized that if he could be of any further assistance, she shouldn't hesitate to call him. He warmly shook her hand, wishing her well.

****

"Please watch out for the shards of glass when going through the car, Miss," the impound attendant warned as he led the two ladies to where the Cadillac was parked.

Shocked at the sight of the severely damaged vehicle, Katelyn gasped, grabbing Cheryl's arm for support. When she was finally able to catch her breath and speak, her voice trembled. "My God, Cher, it's worse than I expected!"

Katelyn's heart was pounding as she approached the vehicle. *Be strong, Kate, be strong,* she kept telling herself, although she found it extremely difficult to suppress the sobs pushing up into her throat.

The driver's side door and section of roof were totally crushed and pushed into the driver's compartment. The window frame and deflated airbag, draped over the steering wheel, were smeared with blood. There were blood drops on the centre console and dashboard, as well as a large bloodstain on the passenger seat.

The impound attendant opened the front passenger door. Katelyn quickly looked inside the glove box and retrieved her mother's favourite music CDs from the centre console. Her sight was now blurred; she had lost the struggle to hold back the tears. *Dear Mom,* Katelyn thought, wiping each eye, *you must have been so afraid.* Her hands shaking, Katelyn pulled the set of keys from her purse and walked to the rear of the car to open the trunk. Her father's golf clubs were still inside, the last Christmas gift from her mother before he died. The cruel reality that both her parents died far too young hit Katelyn like a sledgehammer, and she could no longer stifle the sobs.

****

Driving back to town, Cheryl Miller looked over at her friend who was staring out the car window, deep in thought. She had no intention of leaving her best buddy all alone after the horrific day they had just experienced. She had an idea.

"Hey, Katie, what do you say we pick up the biggest bottle of wine we can find, go back to your place, order a pizza and get drunk?"

Katelyn looked over at Cheryl and managed a smile. "Sounds good to me."

"Good! I'll call Scott and let him know he's taking care of the kids tonight."

Sitting on the den floor in the Ross home, her mouth stuffed full of deluxe pepperoni pizza and feeling the effects of two glasses of wine, Cheryl looked around the room. "Geez, Katie, sitting in here brings back a lot of memories: you and me giving each other manicures, trying new hairstyles and make-up, learning new dance steps. We replayed Madonna's Vogue video so many times trying to get the moves just right, it's a wonder your parents didn't throw us out of the house!"

Katelyn nodded and smiled, busily plucking the green peppers off a slice of pizza. "We would fantasize about boys we had crushes on and cry over boys we broke up with."

Amused, Cheryl watched her friend pick at her food. "Since when did you stop liking green peppers?" Without waiting for a response, she said, "Speaking of break-ups, I don't suppose you've seen Adam Wilson since you've been back."

Katelyn replied, "I have never liked green peppers and no, not yet. How is he?" Satisfied her pizza slice was totally pepper-free, she took a bite.

Cheryl whistled in a wolfish tone. "Girlfriend, he is one hot, and I mean *sizzling* hot boy!"

Katelyn almost choked on her food as she burst out laughing. If anyone knew how to lift her spirits, it was Cheryl.

Katelyn had dated Adam Wilson through high school and university. Their parents were best friends and always hoped that a wedding would take place someday. At that time, Katelyn wasn't looking to settle down and their relationship was getting stale. She had studied hard to be an architect and her career was important to her. When she was offered an excellent paying position in Vancouver, the idea of starting a new job in a city across the country was exciting to her. Adam was hurt and angry that she would even entertain the idea of breaking their relationship to go after a job.

"What the hell are you doing, Katie?" Adam had said. "If you want the excitement of a big city, go look for a job in Toronto!"

"Come with me, Adam," Katelyn replied, trying hard to convince him. "I'm sure there are lots of prospects in the financial industry out there. Just think about it. We'd have a great time together!"

Adam had wanted no part of it. His expression and response were steely. "I'm not going anywhere with you. My life is here."

This was the personality trait that irritated Katelyn the most about Adam. He was stubborn and unmovable; it was his way or no way. She certainly wasn't going to let anyone hold her back in her pursuit of a career. To this day, she didn't regret her decision. It had been almost seven years since she walked away from their relationship and boarded the plane to British Columbia. She held no animosity toward him. Her mother had kept her informed of any new developments with Adam and the Wilson family over the years. He was her parents' financial investment broker and would meet with them at least twice a year when he wasn't running into them on the street.

Katelyn wiped her mouth with a napkin. "I'm not really looking forward to seeing him considering how things were left. The topic is bound to surface at some point."

Cheryl refilled both wine glasses. "Maybe this will be an opportunity to patch things up."

## Chapter Two

Driving the short distance from his condominium situated on the Niagara River to St. Mark's Church, Adam Wilson's thoughts settled on Katelyn. He had been out of the country when she returned to Niagara-on-the-Lake for her father's funeral. How would she receive him after seven years? Would she be warm? Aloof? He parked the black Hummer on the street adjacent to the church. Straightening his black silk tie and buttoning the jacket of his black Hugo Boss suit, he made his way up the walk to the historic building. Stepping through the doorway into the sanctuary, he spied Katelyn at the front of the church standing next to the rose draped coffin, quietly talking to the minister. Sunrays streamed in from all directions through the tall stained glass windows, surrounding her like a spotlight. The oak church pews were filled with townspeople, and as Adam walked up the aisle, he stopped momentarily to shake hands with several of them.

Upon reaching Katelyn's location, he hugged her warmly. "Katie, my God, what can I say? I'm so sorry."

Returning his embrace, she replied, "Thank you for coming, Adam. It's good to see you."

Adam grabbed her hands and held them tightly. Highlights of gold and bronze, reflected by the sun, shimmered throughout Katelyn's shoulder-length hair. Adam studied her face, his eyes lingering at her mouth, and wondered how many thousands of times he had kissed those luscious lips. He felt a sexual stirring as the memories of making love with her came rushing back. Whatever resentment he had felt toward Katelyn when she moved to British Columbia was in the past. Life goes on.

For Katelyn, his appearance had changed dramatically since the last time they saw each other. His mop of sandy blonde hair was cut short, and he had grown a goatee. She remembered his hazel eyes always changed colour depending on what he was wearing, and this day they had taken on a grayish hue to reflect the darkness of his attire. A gold and diamond ring sat on the last finger of his perfectly manicured hand. Cheryl's words echoed in her mind: *he is one hot boy!* Katelyn agreed. She had never seen him looking so good.

He gave her a sympathetic grin. "I'm just so glad I could be here for you. You look wonderful."

"Thank you. I almost didn't recognize you walking up the aisle. The goatee suits you."

"Thanks." As Adam flashed a smile, Katelyn noticed his perfectly straight teeth. *Veneers*, she thought. *Hard to believe this used to be the guy who was happy just wearing jeans, a t-shirt and running shoes.*

Their conversation shortened by others wishing to pay their respects, Adam assured Katelyn he would be in touch to discuss her mother's investment portfolio. He took a seat in the pew next to his parents. Joy Wilson gave him a knowing smile and patted his hand.

"What?" Adam asked, seeing the look of approval on her face.

"She's just as beautiful as ever, don't you think?"

"Yes, mother, she is."

"You know, honey, she could probably use a strong shoulder over the next little while."

"Meaning?" Adam knew exactly what his mother was hinting at, but played along.

"Well, you could be her support; the person she goes to for comfort. Who knows? Maybe she'll realize the mistake she made leaving you and the love of our family all those years ago and decide to stay. Situations can change given the right circumstances."

Adam leaned over and gave his mother a kiss on her cheek. "I'll see what I can do."

****

Katelyn peered out the kitchen window into the backyard; the warm early spring day was beckoning her. The last remnants of snow had disappeared. Crocuses and hyacinths peeked through the ground eager to feel the sun's warmth, while robins, the ultimate indicators that spring had indeed arrived on the Niagara Peninsula, trilled songs of a new season and new beginnings. Almost a week had passed since the funeral and Katelyn had barely ventured outside during that time. Her only travels included two meetings with her mother's lawyer and dinner at Cheryl's home. Making a trip to the grocery store wasn't necessary. Joy Wilson had stopped by early in the week with enough homemade food to last a month.

"I just thought I'd pop in and see how you're getting along," Joy had said, placing a large box in Katelyn's arms.

Peeking inside at the assorted Tupperware containing casseroles, salads and desserts, Katelyn replied happily, "Thank you. That is so sweet of you." Joy was an exceptional cook and Katelyn knew she was in for a real treat. "Please come in for a cup of tea."

"All right," Joy said, following Katelyn into the kitchen. "We really haven't had a chance to talk since the funeral."

As Katelyn placed the food containers in the refrigerator, Joy filled the kettle with water and plugged it into the electrical outlet. "There are some lemon squares in that yellow one, dear. Let's have a couple with our tea."

"Excellent idea!" Katelyn agreed.

Once the tea had been prepared and the squares placed on a serving plate, the ladies sat down at the kitchen table.

"It seems so strange without your mom here," Joy remarked, placing a napkin in her lap.

Katelyn poured a small amount of tea in a cup to check the colour. "Yes, I keep thinking she's going to walk through the door at any moment," she replied with a sigh. "I've heard other people make that comment after losing loved ones, but I never really understood until now." She changed the subject, determined not to cry. "So, how does Ron like retirement?" Satisfied the beverage had steeped long enough, she filled the cup and passed it over to Joy.

"Oh, he likes it fine. I'm the one who's finding it difficult to adjust. And now Abby has moved back in since leaving her husband in January. Married less than five years and already they're talking divorce." Joy shook her head before biting into a square. "I returned to work just to get out of the house and regain some sanity."

Katelyn smiled as she poured a cup of tea for herself. Joy was still the dominant and outspoken member of the Wilson family. She was petite in stature; her salt and pepper hair had been styled the same way for as long as Katelyn could remember. She wasn't one to wear a lot of make-up. She didn't need to. She had a natural beauty, and except for a few laugh lines at the corners of her blue eyes, her skin was flawless.

"You'll have to come over for supper one evening, Kate. I'll arrange for Adam to join us and we'll have a nice family get-together, like we used to."

"I would like that, Joy. Thank you." Katelyn had tried to sound enthusiastic.

"So, what do you think of the new Adam? Quite a change, eh?"

"Yes, I must say he looks quite sophisticated."

"The girls are falling over themselves lining up to go out with him, although he hasn't been able to settle down with anyone since you left. I don't think he has found a girl who can make him happy like you could. He's a very successful businessman and well respected in town. Here, dear, take one." Joy pushed the plate of squares closer to Katelyn. "Are you seeing anyone?"

"Uh, no, not at the moment." Katelyn had easily caught on to what Joy was up to. She didn't think Adam would be too happy if he knew his mother was pitching his assets. Katelyn wasn't there to pick up where she left off all those years ago. She planned on being in town long enough to take care of her mother's affairs, then return to her own successful career and happy life. "Mmm, Joy, these squares are wonderful. You must give me the recipe before I return to Vancouver."

"Yes, of course, Kate."

By the flat tone in Joy's voice, Katelyn knew her last comment had hit its mark.

Returning her thoughts to the present, Katelyn made the decision to take a walk through the town to clear her mind and get reacquainted with the old sights. She loved Niagara-on-the-Lake. It was a town steeped in history, lovingly preserved. Many of the structures built in the late 1700's and early 1800's were still standing, painstakingly restored over time. This was where her love of architecture originated. Any time Katelyn returned home, she would walk up and down the streets of the town, studying the architectural styles of the buildings in front of her.

Although there were plenty of baked goods at home, she couldn't resist stopping by the bakery to purchase a danish. The shop had been in business for decades and it was a favourite stop for the Ross family. After chatting a few moments with the owner, Katelyn left the bakery and continued on her way down Queen Street. Her mouth watering, she pulled the pastry from the small brown paper bag and took a bite. She closed her eyes as the buttery pastry, raspberry filling and sweet icing melded together in one glorious taste. Katelyn had yet to find a bakery in Vancouver that made a homemade danish as delicious. Eating the pastry and admiring a black dress displayed in one of the shop windows, she didn't pay any attention to the Hummer that had pulled up beside her.

"Hi there! Headed anywhere in particular?"

Startled, Katelyn turned toward the direction of the voice. It was Adam. Gingerly wiping the corners of her mouth with her fingers, she walked up to the window of the massive vehicle and peered in. "Just gradually making my way down to Queen's Royal Park before stopping at the cemetery."

"Want a lift?"

Katelyn shrugged. "Sure, why not? Do you have a ladder?" Katelyn managed to hop into the passenger side and looked around the interior. She nodded her head approvingly. "Nice wheels."

"Thanks," Adam replied.

"It's past 10:00. Why aren't you at work?" she asked as she glanced at her watch.

"I had some errands to run," he grinned. "Besides, when you're your own boss, you can work, or not, whenever you like!"

Within minutes they arrived at the waterfront park.

"Thank you, Adam," Katelyn said as she unclasped the seatbelt.

Adam placed his hand on her arm before she opened the door. "So, Katie, how are you holding up?"

She gave him a reassuring smile. "I'm doing okay. Your mother stopped by three days ago with a ton of food and has called a couple of times to see if I need anything. God bless her, she's such a sweet lady."

"Ya, Mom thinks the world of you. She still believes someday we'll get back together, marry and give her beautiful grandchildren!" Adam laughed, half-heartedly.

Although Katelyn wasn't in the mood to revisit such a sensitive topic, she nodded politely and replied, "I'm sure both our mothers spent many hours discussing wedding plans."

After an uncomfortable pause for both of them, Adam asked, "So, how long are you staying in Niagara?"

"At least three weeks. I really haven't gotten that far in the planning process. I'm still trying to wrap my head around the fact that both my parents are gone." Katelyn's voice quivered, her eyes brimming with tears.

Adam took her hand in his. "I'm sorry. I didn't mean to upset you."

"It's all right." She sniffled, reaching into her coat pocket for a tissue. "It doesn't take much to set me off these days!"

"Why don't we go out one evening next week and talk about old times? Have a few laughs."

Katelyn hesitated. In her sad and pensive frame of mind, was she up to spending a couple of hours making conversation and trying to avoid the bringing up of past differences?

****

"Hello Kate! How are you getting along?" Dan was pleased to hear Katelyn's voice. It had been a few days since the last time she called him.

"I'm managing well, Dan. Things are coming together slowly but surely. I've met with the lawyer and the will is currently in probate. There is still the matter of the house and furnishings. I'm hoping to list the house in the next four weeks. The weather will be warmer then."

"Sounds like you've got the situation well in hand." Dan admired her strength, knowing she was an only child with limited emotional support. He was from a family of six children and couldn't imagine facing the loss of his parents without the support of his siblings.

"In the meantime, I was hoping I could work on a few projects from here. My mother has a computer and enjoyed exploring the web so internet access is available, and I brought my laptop. I'm anxious to finish up the RiverVale presentation and start on the Carrington plans."

"Sure, Kate, if you feel up to it."

"I do. Actually, I'm going a little stir crazy and work will be just the remedy."

"Okay. Let me know if there's anything you need. There's nothing we can't email or courier to you."

After chatting a few moments about the weather and bringing Katelyn up to speed on events at the office, Dan bid her goodbye. Trying to focus on the expense sheet he had been working on before Katelyn called, his thoughts continued to stray back to her and their conversation. Realizing she would be away for at least another month, disappointment swept over him. Albeit wishful thinking, Dan had hoped her return would be sooner than that. The office just wasn't the same without her.

## Chapter Three

"You look lovely, Katie," Adam said as they were escorted through the dining room to a small table in front of a window.

Katelyn was dressed in a light gray pant suit and white beaded camisole. Her hair was styled in an up-do, and she finished the ensemble with her mother's pearl necklace and drop pearl earrings. "Thank you. You look quite nice yourself."

Nice was an understatement. Katelyn noticed how well the dark blue suit fit Adam's physique, and the crisp white shirt with button-down collar accentuated his tan. His Giorgio Armani tie was navy with a black stripe. A gold Rolex watch adorned his wrist. He wore a gold and diamond cluster ring on the ring finger of his right hand. This night, Adam's hazel eyes had a bluish tinge to them.

"And thank you," he said, flashing that gorgeous smile.

The server approached the table. "Would you care for something from the bar?"

Katelyn was feeling nervous and apprehensive. Maybe a drink would settle her nerves. Before she had the opportunity to order, Adam responded, "Yes, the lady will have a glass of chardonnay, and I'll have a Chivas on the rocks." Meeting her gaze, Adam knowingly grinned at Katelyn.

"You remembered," she said, trying to remain blasé, even though she was indeed pleased at his recall.

"Of course. Seven years isn't that long a time to forget."

"Do you remember anything else?" she teased.

"Uh, let's see," Adam said, tapping his index finger against his lips. "You love gerber daisies and chocolate truffles, and you won't eat lamb or veal. Oh yes, and your favourite breed of dog is springer spaniel."

"Very good." Katelyn smiled broadly. She was beginning to feel more comfortable and definitely liked the new and improved Adam Wilson sitting across the table from her. *My God, he's delicious!*

"Okay, your turn," Adam said.

"Umm, let me think." Katelyn pretended she needed a few seconds to remember when in fact she had never forgotten. "Your favourite car is a Porsche Carrera, you hate brussels sprouts, and somewhere down the road you switched drinks, because all the time we were together you always ordered screwdrivers."

Adam nodded. "Well done. Although, the Porsche can be removed from the list because I now drive one!"

His mannerism reminded her of a little boy proudly announcing ownership of a coveted toy. Katelyn couldn't help laughing, and said, "A Hummer and a Porsche – sweet! You'll have to take me for a ride in it sometime."

"For you, anytime." Adam studied her face, thinking how little she had changed in both appearance and mannerisms, and how comfortable he felt being with her again.

By the time dessert came, the pair were openly talking and laughing, completely enjoying each other's company.

Earlier that evening, Katelyn had walked to the restaurant and met Adam there; however, when they left almost three hours later, Adam insisted on driving her home.

"I had a nice time, Adam," she said, hugging him before exiting the vehicle.

"So did I, Katie. Maybe we can do it again soon."

****

"How was your evening with Adam? Tell me *every little detail*, don't leave anything out. I want to live vicariously through you, if only for a few minutes." Cheryl and Katelyn took their lattes to a table in the far corner of the coffee shop, away from distractions and eavesdropping patrons.

"I had a nice time," Katelyn replied.

"Where did you go for dinner?" Cheryl sat forward in her chair, totally focused on what her friend had to say.

"The Charles Inn."

"The Charles? Pretty romantic setting for a couple of friends catching up on old times." Cheryl grinned, eyebrows raised.

Katelyn ignored the comment and facial expression. "I had forgotten how elegant that place is. The furnishings are beautiful, and the colours are so typical of that era. The walls were—"

"Okay, okay, enough about the décor already!" Cheryl interjected. "Get down to the juicy stuff. What did the two of you talk about?"

"We reminisced mostly." Katelyn sipped her latte, knowing this wasn't what her friend wanted to hear.

"Reminisced?"

"Ya, about our parents, friends, how the town has changed over the years. Oh, I must tell you, the dinner was absolutely superb. I had the arctic char, and Adam had the beef tenderloin. We chose the crème brûlée for dessert."

"Terrific," Cheryl replied, flatly. "So, how long were you there *reminiscing?*"

"Almost three hours."

"Wow! That's a long stroll down memory lane. Did you talk about how much you missed each other?"

"No!" Katelyn retorted. "Why would we?"

Cheryl continued to prod. "Then what?"

"Then we drove back to my place and that was it."

"Did you invite him in for a coffee?"

"Nope."

"Did he kiss you goodnight?"

"We hugged."

Cheryl scowled. "So much for living vicariously through you. *My life is more interesting.*"

****

Adam arrived at his office feeling tired and irritable. After dropping Katelyn off at the Ross home around 10:00 the previous evening, he drove to his girlfriend's St. Catharines apartment, definitely in the mood for sex. Tanya was a twenty-four-year-old registered massage therapist who had an incredible pair of hands, among other things, and welcomed him any time of the day or night. On this occasion, she helped satisfy Adam's sexual appetite well into the early morning hours.

Sitting at his desk, he downed two aspirin followed by a mouthful of coffee. Picking up the telephone on the third ring, he said, "Adam Wilson."

"Mr. Wilson, it's Sergei Andrakov."

"Yes, sir. How are you?" Adam closed his eyes and rubbed his brow.

"Very good. I'd like to meet with you today to discuss some business."

Adam looked at his calendar; only two appointments scheduled. "I have a pretty hectic day, Mr. Andrakov."

"I'm sure you can make some time to see me. Meet me at Donnlann's Bar at 2:00."

Before Adam could respond, the call was disconnected. "Fuck!" He slammed the telephone receiver back down in the cradle.

****

Born Alexander Petrov in Leningrad, Russia, Sergei Andrakov grew up in an environment of poverty and violence. He was raised by his alcoholic mother and her endless string of boyfriends, most of them unemployed, all of them abusive. Learning how to fight and survive on the streets at a young age, he had become well known to the police by the time he turned sixteen. He continuously searched for ways to unleash his hatred and rage, whether it was by brutalizing the homeless, torturing stray animals or vandalizing property.

Partial to hanging around dark alleyways, one late autumn evening he happened upon one of his abusers who was extremely intoxicated and barely able to stand. Alexander walked up to the man and pushed him against a brick wall.

"Well, look what the rats dragged out," he smirked. "It's been a long time." The drunk studied Alexander's face with no recognition. "Oh come on, don't tell me you've forgotten?" Alexander lifted up the sleeve of his shirt to reveal numerous circular scars dotted along the length of his arm. "Lucky for you I don't smoke." He pulled a switchblade from his back pocket and held it directly in front of the man's face. "Instead, I'm going to make this quick." As panic appeared on the drunk's face and he attempted to cry out, Alexander drove the knife up and under the man's left rib cage. Quickly pulling it out, he could hear air escape from the wound. Staring into his abuser's eyes and smiling sardonically, Alexander felt an overwhelming sense of power as he wielded the knife once more, this time jamming the blade into the right lung. He felt the warmth of the man's blood envelope his hand as he pulled the knife partially out and slammed it in again. Taking great pleasure in watching the man die, he then pulled the switchblade completely out, wiped the blood off on his pant leg, folded it up, and slid it into his coat pocket. He whistled as he walked out of the alley.

A hardened criminal by the age of twenty-one, Alexander obtained a counterfeit passport and, under the guise of a Russian Jew named Sergei Adrianov, immigrated to the United States in 1972. He quickly resumed a life of crime on the streets of New York City, which eventually led to ties with organized crime as a drug runner, then contract killer.

Moving to Canada in 1993, he changed his name to Sergei Andrakov and invested in several shady businesses around the Niagara Peninsula. By the turn of the century, he was head of an organized crime ring involved in prostitution, money laundering, and smuggling stolen, high-end vehicles into the United States.

His relationship with Adam Wilson began when he met the verbose and cocky young man during a high stakes poker game. They conversed between hands, and Andrakov soon learned of Wilson's profession. He was interested in investing a substantial amount of money, and needed an investment professional who could give him the personal attention he required. They agreed to meet the following day at Wilson's office.

"Well then, Mr. Andrakov, how much money were you planning to invest?" Wilson had asked, sitting back in his chair.

"Fifty thousand dollars," replied the Russian. He removed a thick envelope from his inside jacket pocket and placed it on the desk in front of Wilson. "You can count it if you want to."

Wilson picked up the envelope and looked inside.

"And I will pay you ten thousand dollars to keep this just between you and me." Andrakov pulled out another envelope, holding it up for Wilson to see.

Wilson's eyes narrowed and he cleared his throat. "What do you mean, sir, between you and me?"

Andrakov smiled. "Mr. Wilson, I am aware of your obligations as an investment broker to report large cash investments to the government."

FINTRAC, the Financial Transaction and Reports Analysis Centre of Canada, was an independent government agency that partnered with law enforcement groups in the detection and prevention of money laundering. Adam Wilson was obligated to report any suspicious transactions where cash of ten thousand dollars or more from a client was invested.

"So, you also know that should I choose not to report this, I can be charged with a criminal offence."

Andrakov nodded. "I am aware of that; however, this isn't the only investment I plan on making with your firm, Mr. Wilson. The money you could earn through bonuses and commissions would be substantial. It's a very lucrative proposition." Andrakov studied the young man's face. If his hunch was right and Wilson was typical of every other flashy young man he previously recruited—addicted to gambling and heavily in debt—the offer would be too good to pass up.

****

Donnlann's was the type of bar Adam hated to patronize. It was run-down and dark, and the smell of stale beer hit him the moment he walked in the door. The patrons were seedy and raucous—not the type Adam cared to be around—especially if they thought you had money. As his eyes adjusted, he could see Sergei Andrakov sitting in a booth located at the back of the establishment, talking to someone in the seat across from him. Adam guessed Andrakov was in his mid to late fifties judging by his gray hair, sunken eyes and rugged complexion. He had a thick Russian accent but grasped the English language well. He also had a charming personality and was very good at the art of persuasion. As Adam walked to the back of the bar he glanced at the baseball game being broadcast on the large screen television. The Blue Jays were ahead of the Red Sox by two runs in the third inning. Bob Seger's voice blared from stereo speakers hanging from the rafters.

"Mr. Wilson, it's good to see you again." Andrakov stood and extended his hand. "Let me introduce you to my friend, Nickolas Turgenev."

Adam shook Andrakov's large stubby hand, his face void of any expression. He then looked in Turgenev's direction and nodded. *Shit, this bastard is ugly! He not only looks like a bulldog, he's a prime candidate for a heart attack. It's a wonder he could fit inside the booth.* He took a seat beside Andrakov. When the waitress approached, Adam waved her off. He didn't want to spend any more time with these men than he had to.

"So why are we here, sir?" Adam asked.

"Are you sure you don't want something to drink, Mr. Wilson? Scotch maybe? I'll put it on my tab—"

Adam put up his hand while trying to stifle his impatience. "No, no thank you."

Andrakov shrugged. "Very well. I'll get to the point. Nickolas would like to partner with us in our business venture. Isn't that good news?"

*Good news, my ass.* Frowning, Adam began to protest. "Mr. Andrakov, I'm really not in a position to take on any more clients."

Andrakov's steely gray eyes narrowed. "Mr. Turgenev is quite enthusiastic to partner with us. I assured him you would be more than happy to work with him. Besides, what is one more client?"

Adam looked at both men and knew his objections would be futile. You didn't disappoint a man like Andrakov. He forced a smile and replied, "All right. Mr. Turgenev, welcome aboard. When do you wish to finalize the deal?"

"This evening at your place of business, say 10:00?"

"Fine. Now if you'll excuse me, I'm late for another appointment." Adam rose to his feet, shook their hands and quickly left the bar.

That evening Adam again accepted fraudulent identification documents and thirty thousand dollars to set up various investment accounts for Nickolas Turgenev. Adam would deposit the cash in his company bank account in small increments, and later transfer the funds to the investment company on Turgenev's behalf, along with the fraudulent application. Like Andrakov, Turgenev paid Adam ten thousand dollars for not notifying FINTRAC.

## *Chapter Four*

The rainy afternoon hours quickly passed as Katelyn sat at the kitchen table and looked through album after album of photographs memorializing her parents' wedding and honeymoon, trips the little family took together every summer, Christmas holidays, and a large, overstuffed album of pictures representing Katelyn's life from infancy through to her university graduation. She chuckled at the photos of her and Adam taken the night of their senior prom. He looked so uncomfortable in his rented tuxedo.

Katelyn let her mind wander to that night at The Charles Inn. She had enjoyed spending time with Adam again. Although she wanted Cheryl to think it was just an okay evening, it was more than that. Katelyn was surprised how easy it was to fall back into the old relationship with him. He made her feel totally at ease. They laughed and teased, as though seven years and bad feelings had never passed between them. There was no doubt that time had healed their old wounds, as the entire evening was void of any negative feelings or memories.

She had spoken with him on the telephone a couple of times since that evening, but found herself wanting to see him again. She picked up the Shaw Festival Theatre ticket package her mother had left tucked away in the bureau drawer. It had been a Christmas present from

Katelyn to be used when the theatre season started in April. The tickets would go unused unless Katelyn gave them away or attended herself. Would Adam possibly be interested in seeing a production with her?

****

Adam glanced at his Rolex as he and Katelyn left the Shaw Theatre. He wasn't ready to call it an evening just yet. "Say, Katie, it's only 10:00. Would you like to come back to my place for a drink? I'll give you a tour of my condo."

Katelyn wasn't ready to say good night either. "I'd like that."

The mid-April evening was mild, and the couple strolled the few short blocks to Adam's condominium building. Entering the foyer of his unit, the first thing Katelyn saw across the room were floor-to-ceiling sliding glass doors that opened to a large balcony. Lights from Fort Niagara, across the river on the United States shoreline, twinkled in the black night. "Look at that view! The sunsets must be spectacular from here."

Katelyn loved the condo's open layout, with a long marble bar separating the kitchen from the living area. Brown leather couches and dark wood tables were situated in front of a gas fireplace. The walls were painted in terracotta and the area rugs added splashes of colour to the maple hardwood floors. The style was bold, masculine and sophisticated. She couldn't hide her surprise. "Adam Wilson, the décor is stunning! The colours are so vibrant. Did you decorate this room yourself or did you hire an interior designer?"

"Both actually. I hired a designer to lay out the floor plans and contract out the work, but I was very specific on the colour schemes and furnishings."

This was an entirely new side of Adam that Katelyn had never seen before. The Adam Wilson from years gone by would have been happy with furniture from a second-hand store. "Well, you're just full of surprises, aren't you?"

"Wait until you see the master bedroom." A devilish grin crossed Adam's face as he pulled the cork from a bottle of chilled chardonnay. He brought it and two wine glasses over to the leather couch where Katelyn was sitting comfortably with her shoes off and feet tucked underneath her.

"Why don't we save that for another time?" Katelyn felt her cheeks flush and was annoyed with herself for behaving like such a schoolgirl. She quickly steered the conversation in another direction. "From the looks of things, you're doing extremely well in the world of finance."

"Yes, my clients keep me quite busy."

"What do you enjoy the most about your job?"

"Probably helping my clients achieve their dreams, such as retiring early, buying a house or saving for a trip they've always imagined taking. People work so hard to support their families and pay taxes that at times they also forget to pay themselves."

Katelyn nodded, sipping her wine. "We tend to get caught up in the present and don't realize that by investing early, our lifestyles will improve substantially in the long term."

"Exactly."

"Speaking of trips, you're sporting a nice tan."

"Ya, I spent the first two weeks of March in the Cayman Islands, scuba diving and deep sea fishing among other things. I try to vacation there a couple of times a year. And what about yourself? Do you still have a taste for adventure?"

"Uh-huh. I was in Italy for two weeks last spring studying the architecture of Florence and Rome. I'm hoping to go back for a longer stay. I have travelled extensively throughout the U.S. and just recently returned from New York City where I was working on plans to restore an old theatre."

"Sounds like you have a very full life and rewarding career. I guess you don't think much about moving back to Niagara." The comment caught Katelyn a little off guard. His expression was innocent enough. Did he want to know if she ever missed him or regretted her decision to move away?

Choosing her words carefully, she replied, "Well, after Daddy died I tried to convince Mom to move out west so we could be closer—there are a lot of pretty little towns dotted around the Greater Vancouver area—but she preferred to stay with friends and familiar surroundings. And you know, I couldn't really blame her. When I offered to move back, she assured me she would be fine and convinced me not to."

Adam was silent as he refilled their glasses. Wishing she knew exactly what he was thinking, Katelyn continued, "I never got the opportunity to thank you for assisting Mom with her finances after Daddy passed. I know she trusted you implicitly, and was grateful to have you as her advisor."

"Your parents were among my very first clients when I started out. They put their faith in me when many other people wouldn't. Believe me, it was my pleasure." Adam reached over and placed his hand on hers. "You know, Katie, I really didn't want our relationship to end as badly as it did. I'm really very sorry for acting so selfish and childish, and trying to make you feel guilty for wanting to explore life on your own."

Katelyn's suspicions left her and she smiled. "That means a lot, Adam. Thank you. We were both young and wanted so much for ourselves back then that neither one of us was willing to concede. I'm sorry too." She gazed into his eyes and was transported back to a time when all she wanted to do was lose herself in them.

"I've thought about you, about us, often over the years. When I remember our times together, it always gives me a warm and comfortable feeling. The love we shared was incredible. I really haven't experienced anything like it since." Adam removed his hand from hers, placed it on her cheek and leaned in until his mouth met hers. He kissed her tenderly, tasting the wine on her lips, but after a few seconds Katelyn pulled away.

"Uh, Adam, I really don't think this is a good idea."

Adam acted as though he was annoyed with himself, and said sharply, "Damn! I promised myself I wasn't going to do that! You're seeing someone. My apologies—"

"No," she interrupted, "I'm not seeing anyone."

He looked surprised. "Then why so apprehensive?"

Katelyn felt a twinge of defensiveness. "Well, I'm not really looking for a complicated relationship, especially considering the short amount of time I'll be staying here."

Shrugging his shoulders, Adam replied, "Who said anything about a complicated relationship? It was just a kiss."

Katelyn gibed, "Come on, Adam! If I remember correctly, you never stopped at one kiss!"

"Okay, okay, you've got me there!" he responded, laughing. "But it doesn't have to be complicated. Just think about it. No strings, just some fun."

Holding her face in his hands, the second kiss was longer and deeper. His tongue stroked the roof of her mouth, sending a quiver throughout her entire body. She sighed as his lips moved to her ear.

"You taste so good," he whispered, then softly kissed her neck before returning to her mouth. Katelyn quickly surrendered to the sensation as her body responded to his touch. She knew she shouldn't let the situation go too far, but couldn't find the strength to pull back. She was enjoying it too much.

## *Chapter Five*

Dan sat at his desk, absently twirling a pen between his long, slim fingers, as he gazed out the window at the lunch hour shoppers hurrying along Robson Street. Kate had been gone almost three weeks. The atmosphere in the office was dramatically different. Her easy-going manner and contagious laughter were definitely absent. She had been on business trips and vacations before, so why was this any different? He was feeling unsettled but couldn't quite pinpoint the reason.

It had been a year since the divorce from his wife, Candace. Even now, he still wasn't used to being single. In fact, he despised it. At forty-one years of age he was free to see whomever he wanted, whenever he wanted. Dan knew many men who would give anything to be in his position. His buddies were constantly trying to hook him up with friends of theirs, friends of friends, sisters of friends—younger and older than him—but most of the time he turned the invitations down. Dating and getting involved in new relationships was the last thing he was interested in at the present time. That is, until tragedy invaded Katelyn's personal life, forcing her to take an indefinite leave of absence.

"Dan?"

Kate's birthday was the following day and Dan wanted her to know he remembered. He would personally call the florist before the end of day. This was something he didn't want his assistant taking care of. She didn't need to know.

"Dan?"

"Ya?"

"Did you hear what I said?"

Dan swiveled his chair back around to face his partner. "No, sorry, Jaz, I didn't."

"Hey man, you seem preoccupied. What's up?" Jaz had been bringing his partner up to speed on the progress of a restoration project he was working on and so far wasn't getting very much feedback. He removed his glasses and looked at Dan intently.

"What would you say if I told you I was considering asking Kate out on a date when she returns home?"

Jaz grinned. He was pleased to hear that Dan was taking an interest in socializing again, and was even more pleased that his friend's interest was focused on Kate. She was intelligent, beautiful, outgoing, and he couldn't believe a young man hadn't snapped her up before now. He wasted no time in answering. "Well, Dan, old buddy, I'd say, what the hell took you so long?"

****

"Flowers for Katelyn Ross?" the lanky young man asked, holding a long white box. Without waiting for a response, he handed it to Katelyn, swung around and bounded down the front steps to the delivery van.

"Thank you!" she called after him before closing the door.

Her first inclination was that they were from Adam. Excited, Katelyn set the box on the kitchen table, removed the pink curling ribbon and lid, and pulled back the green tissue paper.

"Oh my gosh, how beautiful!" she gasped. She reached in the box and lifted one of the coral, long-stemmed roses to her nose. The scent was heavenly. She quickly opened the tiny envelope and was pleasantly surprised. The card read, *'Happy Birthday, Kate. Fondly, Dan'*. She removed a large vase from the dining room sideboard cabinet and filled it with water. Carefully separating and trimming each rose, she placed them in the container and set the arrangement on the dining room table. She stood for a few moments admiring their delicate beauty before heading to the bathroom to prepare for her date with Adam. They had been spending a lot of time together in recent days and their relationship was heating up.

Katelyn took a long shower, using a lavender scented body scrub. Gently patting herself dry, she then closed her eyes while rubbing unscented lotion over her body, imagining it was Adam's hands travelling over her skin. Despite herself, she was anxious to feel his touch again, and this time it would involve much more than long sensual kisses and tender caresses. After applying makeup and styling her hair, Katelyn proceeded to don black lace panties, garters and stockings before stepping into the black dress carefully laid out on the bed. It was the same dress she had admired in the shop window the morning Adam had stopped and offered her a ride. The material was soft and clinging. The plunging neckline revealed just enough to tease. Her simple black leather stiletto pumps were the finishing touch to the ensemble. She examined herself in the mirror. Yes, she was definitely ready.

It was precisely 7:00 p.m. when Adam rang the doorbell.

"Your carriage waits, m'lady!" Adam took Katelyn's hand as they walked to the red Porsche Carrera parked directly in front of the house. He opened the passenger door for her and waited while she positioned herself in the leather seat, her short black dress sliding up her thighs as she swung her legs inside the car.

"You look gorgeous, as usual," he remarked, bending down to kiss her before closing the door and walking around to the other side of the Porsche.

Katelyn looked over at Adam as he got into the driver's seat. "And as usual, you're looking very hot—with and without the car!" She was feeling flirtatious.

Adam laughed as he shifted and pulled away from the curb. "Grazie, mi amor!"

Throughout dinner, Adam couldn't keep his eyes off of Katelyn. She had a different look and demeanour about her this night, more seductive and playful, and he definitely liked what he saw.

During dessert, he remarked with an impish grin, "I *really* like that dress."

"Oh ya?" Katelyn smiled and leaned slightly forward across the table to give him a better view. "What do you like about it?"

"Everything!" Adam's heart was racing; he felt a stirring between his legs. "I can't believe someone as breathtakingly beautiful as you still isn't married?"

Katelyn shrugged. "All it will take is the right person to sweep me off my feet."

"Well, let me say, it is my pleasure to celebrate your thirtieth birthday with you this evening." He reached into the pocket of his suit jacket, pulled out a small box wrapped in gold paper and set it on the table in front of Katelyn.

"You didn't have to get me a gift." She carefully peeled off the paper and lifted the lid of the black velvet box to reveal a pair of white and black diamond earrings, her birthstone. Katelyn's eyes widened and she gasped, "Oh Adam, they're exquisite! Are these black diamonds? I love them. Thank you so much." She quickly removed the hoops she was wearing and replaced them with his gift. "How do they look?"

"Stunning."

Sitting back again in her chair, she peered at him over the rim of her coffee cup. "The night is still young. Shall we continue the celebration at your place?"

Adam laughed. "Oh, absolutely!"

****

Once inside his condo, Adam quickly took Katelyn in his arms and said, "This will be a birthday you will never forget." He kissed her hungrily as she eagerly pressed her body tightly against him.

When they parted lips, Katelyn whispered, "I'm looking forward to seeing that bedroom."

Adam took Katelyn's hand and led the way. The large room had a king size bed situated at one end. A dark wood armoire, leather chair and ottoman were placed at the other end. Numerous signed hockey and football jerseys from famous athletes were encased in acrylic and displayed on the taupe walls. A corner floor lamp cast a soft light upon the room. Adam walked to the sliding glass doors and closed the blinds before making his way to the bed to turn down the covers.

"I can smell the testosterone in this room," Katelyn joked.

Kicking off her shoes and humming, she set one foot on the leather ottoman and lifted her dress so Adam could see her garter. Slowly, she proceeded to unclip her stocking, roll it down her leg, off her foot and, while grinning wickedly at Adam, drop it on the floor. She repeated the exact same movements with the other stocking. Adam was transfixed, watching her every move with keen interest and thoroughly enjoying the show.

At the finish of her little burlesque act, Katelyn walked toward the bed, smiled demurely and reached her arms out to Adam. "Please help me with my dress."

"It will be my pleasure." He unzipped the slinky, black garment and watched it slide off Katelyn's shoulders onto the floor. She turned to face him clad only in a black garter belt and black lace panties.

"My God, you're beautiful," Adam whispered as he pulled her to him and kissed her hard. As his tongue plunged deep into her mouth, Katelyn could feel the whiskers from his goatee rubbing against her face. Adam's hands moved from her shoulders down her arms to her silky, soft breasts.

"You smell and feel wonderful," he whispered. Kissing her ear and neck, his hands continued their journey down to her waist, her hips, her buttocks. Katelyn let out a sigh, her breath quickening. He returned his lips to hers, kissing her ravenously, his hands pushing her pelvis up against him. She could feel the familiar bulge beneath his pants. Breaking away from their kiss, Adam gently guided her back laterally across the bed. After removing her panties and garter, he knelt on the floor, parted her legs and kissed her inner thighs. "Mmm, you taste good too," he whispered.

The sensation Katelyn felt between her legs was intoxicating and she moaned, stretching her arms over her head and arching her back. This man knew every inch of her body, knew what pleased her, and knew how to bring it about quickly. With every stroke of his tongue, Katelyn's arousal reached newer heights. Within minutes she was climaxing, crying out with pleasure. Her body tingling from head to toe, she gasped, "That was incredible!" She remained on the bed a few moments enjoying the after effects of her orgasm while Adam lightly ran his hands over her body. As he rose to his feet and began to undress, Katelyn moved to a kneeling position on the bed and said, "Allow me." She quickly unbuttoned his shirt and pushed it over his broad shoulders. She ran her hands lightly over his chest and down his taut belly until she reached the waistband of his slacks. With the same swiftness, Katelyn unbuckled his belt, unfastened the button and pulled the zipper down before plunging her hands inside his briefs; one hand anxious to grasp the reward between his legs, the other hand massaging his buttocks.

"You haven't lost your touch, baby," he groaned between kisses.

As though fondling Adam was no longer good enough, Katelyn shoved his pants and briefs down toward the floor and pushed her body against his. She could feel his erection just below her navel.

Joining Katelyn on the bed, he took her in his arms and the couple melded together. Her breasts softly rubbed against his chest, a sensation he never tired of. Katelyn kissed his mouth and neck, her hands eagerly exploring his body. She also knew what he enjoyed, and it wasn't long before she shifted positions and straddled Adam. She gently guided him inside her, still wet and slippery from his tongue. They both groaned as she took in his full length, Katelyn arching her back while thrusting her pelvis up and down. Adam was tightly inside her and she could feel herself becoming swollen with arousal. Adam's breathing quickened as he came closer to orgasm. Katelyn was again moving closer as well. They both rose higher and higher, climaxing within seconds of each other.

****

Trying not to wake him, Katelyn carefully rose from Adam's bed, and made her way to the bathroom for a shower. Naked, she momentarily stood in front of the full length mirror, combing her fingers through her disheveled hair. She suddenly realized Adam was standing in the doorway, also naked and aroused, watching her. "Good morning, Beautiful!"

"Good morning. Sleep well?" Katelyn joked. They had spent most of the night making love.

He walked up behind her and wrapped his arms around her waist, kissing her shoulder. "Who can sleep when you're in my bed? Christ, Katie, I just can't get enough of you."

As they watched their reflections, Adam's hands slowly moved up and down Katelyn's body, circling her breasts, nipples and belly. Her skin tingled at his touch. She followed his hands as they moved over her soft pubic mound, then parted her legs. In a teasing manner, they travelled back to her mound, then again to her inner thighs. Katelyn softly moaned as Adam's one hand caressed the soft, wet place between her legs. The other hand moved up her torso and stopped to rub her breasts in swirling motions.

"Does that feel good, baby?" he whispered in her ear. She turned her face to the side and kissed him, welcoming his tongue into her mouth. She could feel his hardness against her buttocks and moved her hips from side to side in a gentle rhythm. Adam slowly and gently inserted two fingers inside her while continuing to caress her with his thumb.

"Oh, Adam, I love that!" Katelyn groaned. The electric sensation she experienced was euphoric.

Adam continued to whisper erotic words in Katelyn's ear while watching her responses in the mirror. She was smiling blissfully, her eyes closed. She was still rhythmically grinding her bottom against him while her one hand gently kneaded his butt cheek. Her other hand rested on top of his as he rubbed her breasts.

Continuing to breathe faster and faster, Katelyn finally exclaimed, "Please come inside me now!"

Adam removed his fingers and quickly thrust his erection inside her. Her initial gasp was followed by a soft moan as she exhaled. They moved closer and closer to orgasm, crying out when it was gloriously achieved.

Breathless, Katelyn turned to face Adam and kissed him before hugging him tightly. "You're quite right. I will always remember this birthday. Thank you."

## Chapter Six

"Your flowers are beautiful. Are they from Adam?" Cheryl bent over the bouquet of roses and inhaled deeply.

"No, they're from my boss." Katelyn answered nonchalantly as she poured two glasses of sugar-free iced tea from a pitcher.

"Really? Your boss?" Cheryl was surprised as well as curious. "Okay, what's going on that you're not telling me?"

"What do you mean what's going on?" Katelyn had no idea what her friend was referring to.

"Katie, dear, the man sent you roses—*coral roses*—and there's how many here? Two dozen?"

"Thirty." Katelyn handed Cheryl the glass of tea and they both sat down at the kitchen table.

"Thirty. Even better. And you're acting like it's nothing out of the ordinary. You never mentioned there was something between you two."

Laughing, Katelyn put her hands together to form a 'T' and said, "Okay, time out! Rewind! Before you get your panties in a knot, I haven't told you about Dan because there's nothing to tell. So he sent me flowers. He's a nice guy and good friend. That's all!"

Cheryl wasn't giving up and looked at Katelyn in exaggerated disgust. "You don't know what coral roses signify do you?" Before her friend could answer, Cheryl yelled, "Hello? Coral roses signify desire!"

Katelyn scowled. "No way! Says who?"

"Look it up on the Internet. You'll see I'm right."

"Why would he do that? We're good friends."

"Why else? Because he's in love with you," Cheryl replied.

Katelyn waved her hand as though her friend's recent comments were hovering in front of her and she was swatting them back across the table. "I have worked with the man for seven years, and I would know if he was in love with me!"

Katelyn had always thought Dan was a handsome male specimen. When she attended the job interview all those years ago, his strikingly vivid blue eyes—framed by the longest black eyelashes she had ever seen—were what she noticed first. He had a deep, soothing voice, perfect for radio; the kind that would send shivers through any woman's body. He was in great physical condition stemming from his love of the outdoors. She knew he was a good and caring soul. She saw on a daily basis how well he treated the people in his employ, and how they responded to him.

Cheryl needed another approach. "Didn't you mention to me once that he was divorced?"

Katelyn nodded. "Almost a year now."

"So, now he's ready to get back in the game! My bet is he's a true romantic and knew the type of message he wanted to send you. Even the number of roses he ordered tells you something. He realizes turning thirty is a significant day in a person's life."

When Dan told Katelyn he was getting a divorce, she was shocked. Although he spent too many hours at the office in an attempt to establish his business quickly, she knew he loved Candace. Dan was that type of person: committed and loyal. In the months that followed, she saw the strain on his face and knew the situation was impacting him hard. Once his divorce was final, Katelyn had hoped he would ask her out. She waited and watched for a sign from him, but it never came. She could have pursued him but was never under the impression he was interested in a relationship with her. Occasionally he would pop into her dreams at night, sexually fulfilling her like no other man could. One thing she knew for certain, his friendship was invaluable to her and she wouldn't risk that for anything.

Katelyn still wasn't convinced. "I don't know, Cher—"

"One last question and I'll drop the subject. How often has he called or emailed you since you've been here?"

"He calls twice, sometimes three times a week, and writes every day. But it's business related."

"Business, ya, right." Cheryl replied, sarcastically. "You know what they say about absence making the heart grow fonder!"

****

The May afternoon sky was a brilliant blue. The lake winds were brisk, blowing at fifteen knots. Adam's thirty-eight foot Hunter sailboat, *Empress of the Lake*, was docked at the Niagara Sailing Club, a stone's throw from his condominium.

Katelyn had never been on a sailboat; however, she had cruised on powerboats in the past so she wasn't worried about getting seasick.

"Ready to ride the waves?" Adam asked as he boarded the boat and took Katelyn's hand to steady her as she stepped on deck.

"Ready, Captain!"

"Here, you're going to need this," he said, handing her a life vest.

As Adam steered the boat under power onto the Niagara River, he started off by explaining the equipment and directional terms. Katelyn learned the large sail was called the mainsail and the smaller sail was the jib. The sails were hoisted up the mast with a line or rope called a halyard. The boom was the long horizontal pole that swung from side to side. The port side of the boat referred to the left hand side, while starboard referred to the right hand side. The front of the boat was called the bow, and the back was called the stern.

Once on Lake Ontario, Adam showed Katelyn how to tack in order to sail upwind, as well as two basic turns when sailing—'coming about', when the bow of the boat is turned through the wind, and 'jibe', when the stern of the boat is turned through the wind.

The entire experience was a feast for Katelyn's senses. Sunlight reflected off the waves creating a lake of glittering white diamonds. The spray on her face felt icy cold and exhilarating; the air smelled clean and crisp. The sails fluttered in the wind as the boat cut through the swells of Lake Ontario with ease. Katelyn felt free and totally relaxed, her mind temporarily uncluttered. She studied the handsome man at the helm. Again, this was a side of him she had never seen before. "I would have taken you for the powerboat type. How long have you been sailing?"

"Oh, I guess about four years now," Adam replied. "One of my clients introduced me to it and I immediately fell in love. Now each year I can't wait for spring to arrive and grow sad when summer ends."

"I can see why you love it. It has a real calming effect. What other surprises do you have up your sleeve?" Katelyn asked, teasingly.

Adam gave her a wink. "Stick around and I'll show you."

After an hour of sailing, Adam lowered the sails, steered the sailboat under power until they reached a secluded area near shore, and dropped anchor. "This looks like a nice private spot," he said, taking Katelyn by the hand and leading her below deck.

She was pleasantly surprised as she looked around the cabin. It was roomy and beautifully decorated, with hardwood flooring and panelling laid throughout.

Adam walked the few steps to the galley and removed two vodka coolers from the fridge.

"Wow! Fridge, range, microwave, double sink. All the comforts of home," Katelyn remarked as she watched him pour the beverages into two glasses he had retrieved from the cupboard.

"Yep," Adam replied. "You could take an extensive trip with this boat and live on it quite easily."

Handing Katelyn her drink, he then walked to the mid-ship area where a dining table with comfortable seating was situated on one side of the cabin, and a television, DVD and stereo system were built into the opposite wall. He turned on the stereo and tuned in a station. The sound of soft jazz filled the cabin.

"I'm loving this." Katelyn smiled, impressed by the layout and décor.

Adam led Katelyn to the main bedroom, or stateroom, at the stern of the boat. Taking the glass from her hand and setting it on the nightstand, he drew her close. "This is the end of the tour." Cupping her face in his hands, he kissed her long and hard.

Katelyn felt a sexual rush and the anticipated throbbing between her thighs. The couple continued to kiss as they began removing each other's clothing. Gently taking Adam's hardness into her hands, she softly caressed him. "Did I ever tell you what an amazing boom you have, Captain Wilson?"

*The Desires Of Opulence*

Adam smiled broadly. "That's the best compliment I've ever received! Thank you." Taking her in his arms, he guided her onto the bed.

Their long and passionate kisses resumed until Adam broke away and slowly moved his tongue down Katelyn's slender neck and shoulder. Arriving at her breasts, she softly moaned as he circled then gently suckled each nipple. He continued his journey down her belly making Katelyn giggle from being tickled. Adam's mouth finally stopped at the sweet spot between her legs. He slid his hands under her buttocks and tilted her pelvis upward. He kissed her passionately as he slid his tongue inside her.

"Mmm, the ultimate French kiss," Katelyn whispered. She was totally consumed by the sensation of his tongue moving in and out, back and forth, and softly groaned, "Oh yes," until unbridled ecstasy swept over her and she cried out, "Oh Adam, this is heavenly!" When her orgasm subsided, his mouth travelled back up her body until he was in a position to penetrate her. She wrapped her legs around him and welcomed every inch of his erection. It wasn't long before he exploded in waves of release.

"What on earth possessed us to end this relationship?" he panted, laying back on the bed, covered in perspiration. "We're awesome together."

Katelyn didn't respond. She didn't want to reflect on the past or give a second's thought to the difficult issues that lay in wait for her back on land. She was content to be in the moment, lying happily in Adam's arms and feeling the afterglow of their lovemaking. For her, nothing else mattered. She fell asleep to the gentle rocking of the boat.

Katelyn awoke to the sensation of Adam's lips softly kissing hers, his tongue tracing the outline of her mouth before plunging deep. She responded eagerly. Reaching out for him, she pressed her body tightly against his. They came together with an intense hunger, their hands exploring each other. Their hips moved in unison, harder and faster, until an explosion of sexual satisfaction washed over them. Adam waited for his breathing to return to normal before rising from the bed and stepping into his jeans. Zipping them up, he said, "I don't know about you, but I'm starving."

"Naturally a stud like yourself has to keep his strength up," Katelyn joked.

Adam chuckled and looked down at Katelyn sprawled out on the bed. Her freckled skin was flushed and dewy, her damp hair clinging to her forehead. She was smiling lazily.

"You're quite the sex kitten yourself," he responded. "Cheese and crackers?"

"I'd love some."

"Coming up." Taking another full length look at Katelyn on the bed, Adam sighed, "Don't go anywhere."

Within minutes he returned carrying a tray containing a plate of brie and cheddar cheeses, a basket of whole wheat crackers and two glasses of chilled white wine.

Sitting up in bed, the cotton sheet covering her from the waist down, Katelyn held the glass of chardonnay in one hand while topping a cracker with a slice of cheese with the other hand.

Joining her on the bed, Adam clinked his goblet with hers. "Here's to us. A stud and a sex kitten. May we never take the art of lovemaking for granted."

"I'll definitely drink to that," she replied, laughing.

With the last cracker eaten and their wine glasses drained, Adam reached out to caress Katelyn's bare breasts. "Is your appetite satisfied or is there something else I can get for you?"

Smiling seductively, Katelyn took his hand and guided it under the sheet to the sensuous spot between her legs. "Depends on which appetite you're referring to."

## *Chapter Seven*

As the weeks slipped by, the third month of Katelyn's leave of absence was beginning. With the Ross estate out of probate, she was able to list the home and arrange, with the assistance of her own financial advisor, the transfer of part of the inheritance into her accounts in Vancouver.

Katelyn's father had always had a keen interest in investments, whether it was stocks and bonds or mutual funds, and his portfolio was substantial. When he died, all assets automatically transferred to her mother, and then, according to her mother's will, to Katelyn as sole heir.

She spent the morning sorting through her mother's investment file, a task she had been putting off for a long while. She found a document entitled, 'Letter of Authorization', permitting Adam Wilson to manage Margaret Ross's entire financial portfolio and make investments on her behalf. The document was signed and dated by both parties almost a year ago. Katelyn wasn't surprised as she and her mother had discussed her mother's intentions, and they both trusted Adam to make sound and qualified decisions.

A stock portfolio statement dated the previous December was also included among the papers. Two items on the document caught

Katelyn's eye. First, the statement was in her mother's name but sent in care of Adam Wilson at his office. Second, the majority of investments were no longer the blue chip stocks her father had preferred because of their stable earning power and dividend payouts. In their place were numerous companies she was unfamiliar with. Logging onto the Internet, she typed in one ticker symbol after another and discovered they were all small cap, start-up technological companies. *Risky choices. Why would Adam choose these stocks to invest in?* She pulled out every document she could find spanning the two-year period, and the change in paperwork from before her father died until the present was alarming. For years her parents were receiving statements every three months directly to the house. After his death, the statements arrived less frequently, and once her mother signed the letter, drastic changes were being made to the portfolio. Hours passed as she scrutinized every financial statement in the folder, and came to the conclusion that her mother had lost close to one hundred and twenty-five thousand dollars in less than a year. Katelyn was dumbstruck.

She picked up the phone and dialed Adam's cell phone number.

"Hi Adam, it's Kate."

"Hello, Kitten. How's your day going?"

"Good thanks. Any chance I could see you today?"

"Sure. I'm free this evening." He detected an edge to her voice. "Is everything okay?"

"I just had some questions in relation to my mother's portfolio. Could you go over some statements with me?"

"Absolutely. How does 7:00 work?"

"That works for me. See you then."

The tension in Katelyn's voice wasn't a good sign, but whatever the problem, Adam was prepared to give her answers, even if it meant lying.

****

Adam arrived at the Ross home a few minutes before seven. As usual, he was fashionably dressed and reminded Katelyn of the male models who strutted their assets on the runways of New York and Paris. He couldn't have looked hotter unless he was standing before her naked. He took off his designer sunglasses and greeted her with a soft, delicious kiss.

"Let's go into the kitchen. The coffee is freshly brewed, or would you prefer a glass of wine?"

"Coffee will be fine."

"Would you like something to eat?"

"No thanks, I just finished dinner with a client."

Adam removed his suit coat and hung it on the back of a kitchen chair before sitting down. Then he loosened his tie and undid the top button of his shirt. He studied Katelyn as she poured the coffee into two mugs and retrieved a carton of milk from the refrigerator. He could tell she was troubled.

She sat down at the table across from him and, within seconds Ashton had jumped into her lap.

Adam chuckled. "Wow, he's really attached to you."

"Ya, Mom gave him a lot of attention. I think he misses that because he has to be every place I am." She scratched behind the cat's ears and he began to purr.

Adam started the dialogue. "So, what questions did you have for me?"

Katelyn handed him a statement before pouring milk into her coffee. "Well, I was going over the stock portfolio and was quite surprised to see the losses Mom sustained over the past year. Daddy had a significant number of blue chip stocks: IBM, Coca-Cola, Johnson & Johnson, General Electric. According to that statement, they've all been sold and replaced with start-up, lesser known companies. Why?"

Adam took a sip of coffee. "I felt it was time she traded them and with the profits she made, reinvest during a time when some stocks were at a better price. The money markets have taken a beating, but will eventually recover."

Katelyn disagreed. "Well, I know for sure that Daddy wouldn't have approved of these investments."

"Katie, your dad wasn't a certified advisor, and your mother trusted me to make investments on her behalf based upon my recommendations. You know I would never intentionally put her money at risk." Adam looked intently into her eyes. "Katie, you do know that?"

Katelyn met his eyes and wanted terribly to believe him. She could hear the tension in Adam's voice, but ignored the question and pressed on.

She handed him another statement. "According to my calculations, Mom lost close to one hundred and twenty-five thousand dollars in just under a year. Now, I don't know about you, but to me, that's a lot of money for someone who wasn't far away from retirement. How could you let that happen?"

Adam's patience had run out. Irritated, he snapped back, "How could I *let* it happen? What the hell does that mean?"

Katelyn saw the anger flash in his dark eyes, but she wasn't backing down. "It means, where did all the money go? It's a simple question."

At this point they were both raising their voices, causing the cat to leap off Katelyn's lap and run down the hall to a safe hiding place.

Adam's eyes narrowed and his jaw began to tighten. "Whoa, wait a minute! You don't trust me, do you?"

"I want to trust you, Adam, but my lord, *one hundred and twenty-five thousand dollars*!"

Adam's facial expression turned from anger to that of extreme hurt and disappointment. "You know, Katie, I thought we had something monumental going on between us these past few weeks." His mouth was twitching. "I had truly hoped our relationship and the awesome love we shared would be enough for you to give up your life in Vancouver and remain here with me. That we would get married, buy a big house, fill it with children and have the fairytale life our parents had wished for us. But I see I'm the only one foolish enough to believe that story!"

Katelyn was surprised by Adam's words. She looked at him incredulously. "Adam, I gave you no indication I was staying."

Adam got up from his chair, took two steps toward Katelyn, grabbed her by the arms and pulled her out of her seat. Standing toe to toe, his eyes burned into hers, his lip quivering.

"Katie, I love you. I have always loved you. It was hell when you left me the first time. Please, don't do it again."

"Adam—" Katelyn tried to interject, but he wouldn't let her speak.

He tightened his grip on her arms and shook her once. "No, Katie, *listen to me*! We can get married and live right here in this house. I know how much you love it. Or we can live in my condo, or buy a home right on the lake. Whatever you want, Sweetheart. If you're worried about your career, we can set you up with a business of your own. We can have a remarkable life together. Can't you see that?"

Katelyn felt the full impact of Adam's desperation and was deeply moved. She couldn't stand to see him so shaken.

"Okay, Adam. Shhhh." She put her index finger to his lips and whispered, soothingly, "It'll be all right. We'll work it out."

She removed her finger from his mouth and kissed him gently. Adam responded hungrily by pulling her close. As always, Katelyn was held captive by his touch, his smell, his taste. His hands travelled under her t-shirt and moved up her back. Katelyn broke the embrace to lift her arms up as Adam pulled the garment over her head. They resumed kissing as she unbuttoned his shirt while he reached down to unzip her shorts and yanked them over her hips. She hurriedly loosened his belt and undid his pants, releasing him from the confines of his clothing and into her gentle grasp. As Adam lifted her by the buttocks, Katelyn wrapped her legs around his waist, and the two lovers connected with one intense thrust.

****

Katelyn climbed into bed, plumping the pillows before settling down to read a stack of letters she had found tucked away in a bureau drawer. The only audible sound throughout the quiet house was Ashton's heavy breathing as he slept next to her. The letters were from her father, his writing large and sprawling across the pages. As she read the words of a young man madly in love and desperately missing his sweetheart, she felt their strength. He was away at university and couldn't afford to travel back home every weekend. He wanted her mother to know that he thought of her all the time, and counted the days until he could see her again. He counted the days until they could marry and never be apart.

Throughout her entire lifetime, Katelyn witnessed that love shared between her mother and father. She remembered how, as a little girl, she would feel jealousy whenever her parents hugged and kissed each other, and would usually butt in between them to break the embrace. As a teenager, she would protest in embarrassment at the slightest demonstration of affection by the couple. It wasn't until she became a young adult, personally experiencing the power of love, that she realized how truly devoted her parents were, and how their love had sustained many years of trials and triumphs. She wanted that for herself, a loving relationship that was everlasting.

The love Adam professed for her earlier that evening played over and over in her mind. She was surprised to hear the passion in his voice and see the pleading in his eyes. She had never before believed in fate, but now she wasn't so sure. Maybe situations did happen for a reason, and maybe she and Adam were meant to be together after all this time. One thing Katelyn knew for sure, she was falling in love with him all over again.

## Chapter Eight

The name *Monica Tran* appeared on the screen of Katelyn's iPhone. Monica was a certified financial planner with a major Vancouver investment institution.

"Hello, Monica. Did you receive the paperwork I faxed you?" Katelyn asked.

"Yes, Kate, I did. I've looked over your mother's investment statements along with your signed transfer form, and I'm deeply concerned."

Katelyn replied, "Oh? By what?"

"Well, I've been in touch with the fund companies listed on the documents, and according to them, there is little or no money in the unregistered fund accounts."

"How could that be?" Katelyn asked.

"The money was withdrawn by Adam Wilson over a period of eight months. Because the mutual funds were unregistered, he would have easy access to those accounts."

"Withdrawn by Adam?" Katelyn's mind was beginning to race. "I don't remember seeing any withdrawals on the statements my mother received."

"That's because they've been omitted. I suspect the statements your mother received were prepared by Adam Wilson, and in that type of situation he would be able to enter or leave out any amounts he wanted. Your mother would never have known how little she actually had in her accounts."

Katelyn's heart began to pound. "Wait, Monica, there has to be a mistake. Adam has been a friend of my family for years. He would never steal money from us."

"Kate, it's not in my best interest to point fingers without the evidence to back it up. The funds your mother owned before she signed the Letter of Authorization are no longer there."

Katelyn closed her eyes and tried to remain calm. "Would you be able to tell me the timeline of the activity. I mean, the date the withdrawals started to the date they ended?"

"Yes. Let's see, the first major withdrawal was July 22nd of last year and—"

"What date was the Letter of Authorization signed?" Katelyn interrupted.

"July 10th."

"And when was the last withdrawal?"

"Um, last withdrawal was this past March. March 30th."

"March 30th? That was two days after my mother died."

There was a pause on the other end of the line. "Kate, it was Adam Wilson's fiduciary responsibility, as your mother's advisor, to freeze those accounts upon notification of her death."

Sickened by what she was hearing, Katelyn felt faint and grabbed the nearest chair before her legs went out from under her.

"Kate, are you still there?"

Almost in a whisper, she replied, "Yes, I'm here."

"Listen to me now. This is very important. My advice is to go to the police. By removing those funds, Adam Wilson has committed a criminal act."

Getting up from the chair, Katelyn quickly thanked Monica for her assistance and disconnected the call. She dropped her iPhone on the kitchen counter and ran down the hall to the bathroom as a wave of nausea hit. After vomitting, she broke down in tears, and continued crying until exhaustion overtook her. Katelyn had never felt so betrayed. Everything her parents had worked hard for their entire lives was gone. How could Adam have done this to them? To her? No wonder he lived so well. He was using other people's hard earned savings to do it. And to think she cared for him, shared a bed with him, considered giving up her life out west to resume one with him here. Katelyn laid on the bathroom floor in the fetal position for what seemed like hours.

****

Katelyn dumped the contents of her purse out on the bed, frantically searching for Sergeant Armstrong's business card.

*"What did I do with it?"* she yelled in exasperation. When she finally located the card tucked inside her new wallet, she called the number, left a message and within half an hour the police officer called her back. Trying to remain calm, Katelyn explained the situation to him. Armstrong transferred her to the Central Fraud Unit where she spoke with Detective Mike Wyatt. After giving him an outline of her complaint, they arranged to meet the following day. She was advised to bring copies of her parents' financial statements from the past two years, as well as any other documentation she had as proof of Adam

Wilson's fraudulent activities. By the time the call had ended, Katelyn was feeling somewhat back in control.

****

"Kate, it's Dan."

"Oh, Dan. I'm sorry I haven't returned your calls."

"You sound exhausted. Are you all right?"

Kate inhaled deeply, trying to keep her composure. "Well, no. By the looks of things, my parents' financial broker has managed to wipe out a good portion of the portfolio. My mother signed a letter giving him control over her investments and he has defrauded her of thousands."

"Christ! How did you find this out?"

"I was arranging to have Monica Tran transfer the funds into my accounts, and she called to tell me the statements were falsified."

"Have you talked to your mother's lawyer about this?"

"No. He's a good friend of the Wilson family, so I don't know how impartial he would be. My first inclination was to call the police. I have an appointment to see a detective in the Niagara Police Fraud Unit tomorrow morning."

Dan was astounded at this woman's courage, considering the adversity she was facing. "You're an extraordinary woman, Kate. Is there anything I can do from this end?"

"Your encouragement means a lot to me, Dan."

"Just remember, Kate, you're never alone. Call me any time, day or night."

His words to her sounded hollow as he hung up the telephone. Should he drop everything and fly to Ontario? Dan's frustration was mounting as he paced back and forth in his office. In the years he had known her, Dan had never heard Katelyn sounding so low. He was sure she had reached her breaking point, her vibrant spirit being suffocated by unfortunate and unforeseen circumstances. Not only was he concerned for her mental and physical well being, his desire to see her was beginning to consume him. Hearing her voice on the phone wasn't enough anymore. Walking over to his desk, he glanced at his appointment book. He had a busy week ahead of him, but most of the meetings could be rescheduled, and Jaz could manage the rest. Dan punched in his assistant's extension.

"Seema, please book me on a flight to Hamilton, Ontario, as soon as possible, and if Hamilton's a no-go, make it Toronto."

## Chapter Nine

Detective Wyatt had been a police officer with Niagara for over two decades, and a detective in the Fraud Unit for eight of those years. He felt badly for the pretty, young woman sitting across the table from him this morning. As she told the detective her story and answered his questions, she fidgeted with the band on her wristwatch. *Christ*, he thought, *it's bad enough to lose a family member, but to be kicked when you're already down by a so-called good friend is despicable.* Wyatt was sure the creep hadn't counted on Margaret Ross dying. In all likelihood the plan was to slowly siphon her accounts dry until there was nothing left. Once he knew of her death, it gave him the perfect opportunity to scoop the remaining funds before anyone discovered what he was doing. The story was sad and all too common.

"I'm hoping, Detective, you can help me make sense of this entire situation. Why do you think Adam would take such a risk when he stands to lose everything?" Katelyn asked.

"Oh, there could be a number of reasons," he replied, laying down his pen and clasping his hands together. "He may be deeply in financial debt, or he may have a drug addiction or gambling addiction. Those are the most common reasons. He could be involved with the wrong people and owes them a great deal of money, or he may have sociopathic tendencies and feels absolutely guiltless about hurting or destroying the people who care for him. Sociopaths are charming people with a talent for lying."

Katelyn nodded that she understood. "How long does it usually take to investigate cases like this?"

"Fraud investigations take anywhere from a few months to a year to complete. In the meantime, I recommend you contact a lawyer to begin a civil suit against Adam Wilson. The courts will be able to seize his assets and bank accounts." Wyatt handed her his business card. "Call me if you have any questions or if there's anything else you think I should be aware of, and I'll do the same. When do you plan on returning to Vancouver?"

"Within the next month. Hopefully I can find a buyer for the house by that time."

"Well, good luck, Miss Ross. I'll be in touch." Wyatt extended his hand.

Katelyn shook it and thanked him for his time.

****

Katelyn changed out of her dress pants and blouse into jeans and a T-shirt. She was tired and depressed. She missed her home and her friends. Adam hadn't come around since their sexual encounter in the kitchen three days ago, and Katelyn preferred it that way. She felt completely violated and emotionally bruised. He had drawn her into an intense relationship at a time when her emotions were raw, then proceeded to deceive her when she found out about his misdealings. What was his motive in rekindling their old romance? Was he truly pleased she came back? She was doubtful. He knew that she would stumble upon his scheme eventually, unless he was able to convince her to marry him, persuade her to let him take over her portfolio and combine her funds with her mother's without her ever knowing about the fraud. She had no doubt he would bleed her dry as well. Katelyn found it difficult to believe Adam had become this type of man. In his early 20's he was self-assured, sensitive and caring. Now he was artificial, devious and money-driven. The thought of becoming his wife and mother to his children sent chills down her spine.

Her thoughts were interrupted by the doorbell, and as she walked down the hall toward the front door, she prayed it wasn't Adam. She didn't have the strength to confront him. When Katelyn saw Dan standing on the porch, her large, green eyes grew even wider. She squealed with delight and threw her arms around his neck. He laughed, enveloping her in his strong embrace and lifting her off her feet. A myriad of emotions erupted inside her. Completely overcome by the sight and feel of him, Katelyn began to sob, her body quivering.

Dan held her tighter and whispered, "Dear Kate, you've been through so much." She buried her face in his neck, not wanting to let go. Releasing her, he took her face in his hands and looked into her tired, pained eyes. Softly he said, "Everything will be all right. You'll see." He smiled and wiped her tears away with his thumbs.

Composing herself, Katelyn took Dan's hand and led him into the house to the living room where they sat down on the sofa. She studied his handsome features and shook her head incredulously. "I can't believe you're here! You don't know how much this means to me. It is so good to see you, Dan."

He squeezed her hand and replied, "I thought you could use a little moral support."

****

The outer office of Gordon Stratton, Attorney, was furnished impressively with black leather chairs and settees, bevelled glass and pewter tables. Large black and white photographs of famous landmarks from around the world were framed in black lacquer and pewter, and hung on grey walls. The look was distinctly masculine.

*The Desires Of Opulence*

While Dan waited in the anterior room, Katelyn followed the assistant into Stratton's private office. He shook her hand warmly and escorted her to one of two chairs facing his mahogany desk. Glancing around the room, she couldn't help but notice how stark it looked. Stacks of files sat on every corner of his desk and on a credenza situated against one wall. A large bookcase sat half full of books, while two boxes sat on the floor waiting to be emptied.

"Excuse the mess," Stratton explained. "I just moved in two weeks ago and haven't been able to find the time to put everything away. I keep rescheduling the interior designer because she needs a few days to decorate, and right now I can't give her that much time. I'm just too busy. Please sit down."

As Stratton returned to his chair, Katelyn noticed a diploma from the University of Western Ontario hung on the wall just above his head. Stratton had a combined degree in legislative law and business administration.

"I hope you'll be able to take my case," Katelyn said.

"Oh yes, that won't be a problem. First of all, my condolences on the loss of your mother."

"Thank you."

Putting on his glasses, the lawyer continued, "I've had a chance to examine the documents you had couriered over. Mr. Wilson has indeed been busy. I've litigated quite a few investment fraud cases over the years, and the telltale signs are all here. When notified of your mother's death, it was Mr. Wilson's duty as her broker to transfer her funds where they would be protected from any fluctuations in the market, then freeze the accounts in preparation for probate. The Letter of Authorization between him and your mother would have expired at that time."

"Instead, he withdrew every dollar he could get his hands on," Katelyn added.

Stratton looked at her sympathetically. "It appears that way. Mr. Wilson was also doing a fair amount of 'churning', meaning he was constantly reinvesting the stocks in order to generate commissions for himself. Have you heard of a group called the Canadian Securities Administrators?"

Katelyn shook her head. "No, I haven't."

"Well, the CSA is a group of securities regulators from every province and territory within Canada, and they conducted a study which revealed that one in twenty Canadians have been victims of investment fraud. Many times the fraud was committed by someone the victim knew and trusted, as in your mother's situation. Because Adam Wilson was a long time family friend and your parents' investment broker for years, there was absolutely no reason why your mother wouldn't trust him. In fact, I'm almost positive that when the police have concluded their investigation, they will find your mother wasn't Wilson's only victim." Stratton paused momentarily to scribble a few notes on his writing pad, then asked, "Have you spoken with the police?"

"Yes, I've met with a detective from the Fraud Unit."

"And what did he say?"

"That there was enough evidence to start a police investigation, and that it would take months to a year to complete. I was advised that in the meantime, I might want to consider seeing a lawyer to start civil action against Mr. Wilson."

Stratton nodded he understood while busily writing.

"So, what are my options?" Katelyn asked.

The lawyer sat back in his chair and removed his glasses. "We can begin a court action against him and his company. I can prepare a petition to have his personal and business bank accounts frozen, as well as any real estate, vehicles, and other assets he may have. The police

*The Desires Of Opulence*

will see to it that his business records are seized during the course of their investigation, at which time I can request copies for our case."

Katelyn smiled at the lawyer, encouraged by his words. Breathing a sigh, she said, "All right, let's do that, Mr. Stratton. Adam Wilson's lavish spending is about to come to a halt."

\*\*\*\*

Katelyn spent the warm and sunny afternoon showing Dan around Niagara-on-the-Lake. The flowerbeds lining the boulevards and sidewalks were bursting with colourful annuals and shrubs. Horses sauntered through the streets, pulling antique carriages carrying passengers who marvelled at the classic architecture of an era frozen in time.

"This is a beautiful little town, Kate," Dan commented as they walked down Queen Street amid the many tourists.

Katelyn nodded in agreement. "I loved growing up here. Generation after generation of families lived and worked in these buildings. As a little girl, I would imagine what the children were like who lived in our house all those years before us. Did they play hopscotch or skip rope on the very same sidewalk I played on? What songs did they sing or books did they read? I began to spend hours in the library researching the town's past residents and visiting their graves in St. Mark's cemetery. I devoured every book I could get my hands on that explained the impact the British, French and American colonies had on our country. My summers as a teenager were spent working as a tour guide at Fort George."

"Hey there, girlfriend!"

Cheryl had just exited the post office and was walking toward them. She reached out to give Katelyn a hug. Looking over at Dan she said, "Who's this good looking gentleman?"

"Cheryl Miller, this is Dan Neufeld."

"Nice to meet you, Dan. Oh wait … Dan Neufeld … Katie's boss?"

Dan smiled and replied, "The one and only. Nice to meet you, too." He extended his hand.

Wide-eyed and grinning broadly, Cheryl turned to Katelyn and said, "Now we can resolve our little discussion by getting the answer straight from the horse's mouth." Then she quickly turned back to Dan. "Not that you look like a horse by any stretch of the imagination!"

Dan was puzzled but amused. "Thank you."

Totally embarrassed, Katelyn frowned. "No, Cheryl, we don't have to resolve it."

Cheryl ignored her friend and put her hand on Dan's arm. "You see, Dan, judging by those exquisite flowers you sent Katie for her birthday, I'm of the opinion that you are knowledgeable in the significance of rose colours and their true meanings. Am I right?"

Dan nodded. "I've ordered a few bouquets in my time."

"Aha!" Cheryl shouted, pointing her index finger at Katelyn. "See, Katie, I told you! I love it when I'm right. So Dan, what brings you here?"

Katelyn had intentionally left Cheryl in the dark about Adam's misdealings, and interjected before Dan could answer. "Cheryl, stop grilling the poor man! Dan's here because I'm always raving about Niagara, so he decided to take some time off and see it for himself."

"I was just commenting to Kate what a beautiful town this is," Dan added.

"Isn't it great? One of Ontario's little gems. You have to visit a winery or two, and, of course, Niagara Falls is a must see." Cheryl glanced at her watch and said, "Oh crap! I better get going. The kids will be getting home from school soon. Enjoy your stay, Dan."

Hugging Katelyn goodbye, she whispered in her friend's ear, "That man flew all this way to see you. You need to wrap things up and get your butt back to B.C.!"

## Chapter Ten

"Hi, Gorgeous! I stopped by to see if you're okay. Why haven't you returned my phone calls?" Walking through the doorway, Adam bent to kiss Katelyn, but she quickly turned her face away from him.

She was still seething and clenched her jaw as she spoke. "What do you care?"

Adam looked puzzled. "What do you mean? I care about you deeply. What's wrong?"

Katelyn couldn't believe the nerve of this man. "Well, for starters, you've stolen money from my parents, as well as from me."

Adam looked shocked. "What are you talking about?"

"Don't play dumb, Adam! You know exactly what I'm talking about! Just like you knew what I was talking about that night I questioned you about the financial statements, and you ran your game about how much you loved and needed me. You have absolutely no intentions of marrying me. All you want is my money, isn't that right?"

"You're not making any sense," Adam retorted.

Katelyn ignored the last remark. "You were like a member of the family. My parents trusted you, I trusted you, and you callously violated that trust. To think you were helping yourself to their life savings right up until the end. While I was grievously making funeral arrangements for my mother and going through her bloodstained car, you took one last opportunity to scoop what funds you could." Katelyn shook her head in disgust. "And all those times we made love, did you feel any remorse? It sickens me; you sicken me!" Katelyn's hands were shaking and her voice was raspy, but she refused to break down in front of him.

"Have you finished your little tirade?" Adam asked with contempt.

Katelyn began to protest, but he held up his hand to stop her. He continued on, "You know, Katie, I think the grief and strain you have been under these past few weeks has seriously affected your judgement. You don't know what you're saying."

"The hell I don't," Katelyn spat. "This conversation is over. Get out!"

As she turned to walk away from him, Adam grabbed her arm and roughly yanked her toward him. His fingers dug deep into her skin causing her to squirm in pain. His face was inches from hers and his eyes were dark and menacing. He snarled, "If you go to the police with this, believe me, you're not going to like the consequences."

"Let go of me!" Katelyn shouted, struggling to break free of his vice-like grip.

"I strongly suggest you take your hand from her arm." Dan's deep voice emanated from the front door.

Startled by the stranger, Adam released Katelyn immediately. She stumbled backward but was able to regain her balance. Dan's intervention sent a wave of relief washing over her.

"Who the hell are you?" Adam snorted, giving Dan the once over.

"A friend of Kate's," Dan replied in a sharp tone. "Now leave."

"Ya, well, this has nothing to do with you, asshole. This is between Kate and me." Adam turned his back to Dan and addressed Katelyn through clenched teeth. "We'll continue this conversation later. In the meantime, don't forget what I said."

"I told you to leave." Dan took two strides in Adam's direction, grabbed him by the arm and tried to forcibly remove him from the house. Adam resisted, taking a swing at Dan with his free arm; however, Dan ducked and came back, driving his fist into Adam's stomach. Groaning, Adam doubled over in pain and clutched his mid-section. Before he could recover, Dan was dragging him out the door and down the porch stairs. "Come back and you'll have to deal with the police."

Adam slowly stood upright, staggered to his car, and yelled an obscenity at Dan before getting in and peeling away from the curb. Dan ran back inside the house and found Katelyn sitting on the sofa, looking pale and trembling. He sat down beside her and put his arm around her. "Are you alright?"

"I'm okay," she replied, rubbing the red welts that were quickly appearing on her arm. "I'm so glad you came by when you did."

"Kate, I think you should call the police. You may have to get a restraining order against that guy."

Katelyn nodded. The look in Adam's eyes had been deeply disturbing. She was convinced beyond any doubt that he was not the man she used to know all those years ago.

****

Adam was recovering on the leather couch in his office when he received a call from Andrakov requesting another meeting. He was now seeing Andrakov and Turgenev twice a month and found it difficult to service his legitimate clients with so many fraudulent accounts taking up his time. To make matters worse, Andrakov was now only paying him five thousand dollars instead of ten thousand to keep FINTRAC out of the picture. *Filthy bastard!* Adam knew there was nothing he could do about it. He was in over his head with no way out. If he went to the police and told them the mess he was in, he would be arrested on a slew of charges including theft, fraud, money laundering and taking part in organized crime. He had no doubt they could find a few more to tack on.

Their meeting took place in the usual booth at Donnlann's Bar. When Andrakov advised him another partner would be joining the business deal, Adam was firm in his refusal to cooperate. Trying to hide his irritation, he remarked, "Mr. Andrakov, you know as well as I do that what we are involved in is illegal. I can't afford to screw up and raise any red flags with the Canadian Securities Commission. If I take on any more business, that's exactly what is going to happen."

The Russian was insistent. "I have full confidence in your abilities and expertise, Mr. Wilson. You will find a way to service me and my two partners."

Adam shook his head. "I must decline, sir."

"That's extremely disappointing," he said, scowling. "I have brought you a lot of business and made you a very wealthy man, and this is how you repay me?"

Adam knew he was playing with fire where this prick was concerned, but he had to take a stand. "My career and reputation are on the line here, not to mention my freedom if I'm caught by the police. That's a hell of a lot to lose."

Andrakov's displeasure was evident. The Russian sat forward in his seat, his deep-set eyes bore into Adam's. "Only if you're caught, Mr. Wilson," he said flatly. "Your situation could be worse. You could lose your life."

Adam's anger had reached the boiling point. His heart was pounding. His fists were clenched under the table, fingernails cutting into his palms. "*Are you threatening me?*" he hissed. Not waiting for a response, he continued, "Maybe I shouldn't wait. Maybe I should make a trip to the police myself. I'm sure they'd be willing to cut a deal with me in exchange for information on you and your little group of friends."

Andrakov smirked. "You wouldn't be that stupid." He rose from the table to leave. "Very well then, Mr. Wilson. I will find someone else to work with my friend."

When he left, Adam remained seated in the booth for another ten minutes. He ordered a double scotch, straight up. When the waitress brought the drink, he downed it in two gulps. Only then did the full impact of what just took place hit him, and he began to shake. *Dear God, what have I done?*

****

The flaming sun had set. Streaks of pink in the sky quickly faded as an indigo twilight descended. Adam drove his Porsche, top down, along the Niagara Parkway in the direction of Niagara-on-the-Lake, his mind racing as he contemplated how to get out of the cesspool he found himself in. *Damn!* If only he hadn't mouthed off to Andrakov. His temper had always been a problem for him and was difficult to rein in most of the time. He knew Andrakov wouldn't shrug off what was discussed at that meeting. The Russian had him by the balls.

Adam glanced down at the dashboard gauges and checked his driving speed. Twenty kilometres over the limit. He eased his foot off of the gas pedal. The Niagara Police had nabbed him twice already this year and he couldn't afford to lose any more points. An amazing piece of machinery like this and he couldn't open it up. *Fucking cops. Another source of irritation.*

His thoughts turned to Katelyn and the events of that morning. He was annoyed that she had managed to go over each financial statement with a fine toothcomb, something her mother obviously never did, and

*The Desires Of Opulence*

now she was on to his scheme. And who was that guy who stormed in on the two of them? Her lawyer? Adam had never seen him around town before. Too bad his fist hadn't connected with the jerk's face. He would have taken great pleasure in laying the guy flat out. He placed his hand on his stomach; it was still pretty sore. A lucky punch.

Katelyn's discovery was the least of his worries. He needed to come up with a plan to rid himself of those Russian dirtbags. Maybe he'd take the Hunter on a trip, disappear for awhile. Yes, the longer he thought about it, the more he liked the idea. To hell with his practice. He would pack, stock up on supplies, and set sail within the next couple of days.

## Chapter Eleven

It was 2:00 a.m. when Adam left Tanya's apartment. He would have preferred to stay with her the entire night, but was setting sail just after 7:00 that morning. He was twenty feet from his car when a black van pulled up and two men jumped out to confront him. One man grabbed Adam's arms from behind while the other shoved a handgun in his face and searched his pockets. Taking Adam's wallet and Blackberry Pearl, he growled to his partner, "No weapons. Grab the keys and take off."

Prying the key ring from Adam's hand, the second man then quickly walked to the Porsche, unlocked the driver's side door and got in. He started the ignition and waited. The gunman pushed Adam into the rear of the van. "C'mon, Wilson, let's take a ride."

Adam tried to resist. "Where the hell are you taking me?"

"Shut up, asshole!" snapped the gunman, hitting Adam with the butt of the pistol. Calling to the van's driver, he said, "Okay, Eddie, let's get outta here!"

Intense pain shot up the back of Adam's head. His neck felt wet and sticky, and he was having difficulty focussing. The van sped away with the Porsche following behind. On the outskirts of St. Catharines the two vehicles parted ways.

"Listen up, shithead," the gunman demanded, yanking Adam's head up by his hair. "We're here to do a little business for Mr. Andrakov."

"What are you talking about?" Adam mumbled, grimacing.

"You know Sergei Andrakov? The man you mouthed off to?"

"I don't know what you're talking about."

"No, of course not. Just shut up and listen! Mr. Andrakov doesn't take kindly to threats. He has dealt with hundreds of *mudaks* like you over the years. Big shots with big mouths and brains the size of their dicks. Well, we'll see what a big man you really are after tonight. We're going to make a visit to your office where you're going to hand over all the cash you've got stashed in your safe. Then we're going to stop by your condo and see just how much loot we can collect there. And if you try anything to attract attention, it'll be the last thing you do."

\*\*\*\*

The gunman stood behind Adam, pressing the pistol into his back. One thug quickly looked through the desk and filing cabinet drawers while Eddie, the van driver, immediately went to the safe.

"We need the code to your safe, Wilson," he called out. "Give it up."

Adam could barely think as he leaned his shoulder against the wall for support. His head felt like it had been split in two. *What was the code?*

Eddie walked over to Adam. "I said, give it up!"

Adam was desperately trying to remember. *What the hell was the code? Seven, four, nine…* His thoughts were interrupted by Eddie's fist connecting with the side of his face. Intense pain ripped through his ear, eye and cheek. Groaning, Adam dropped to his knees. The next blow was a kick to his rib cage. Adam could barely breathe.

"God damn it!" he gasped. "Wait a fucking minute! Seven, four … no … seven, five, nine, three."

The gunman laughed. "Jesus, you really are stupid. What did you think he was going to do? Say pretty please, can I have the code?"

Eddie punched in the numbers, opened the door and scooped the entire contents of the safe into a briefcase. With a nod of his head, the gunman motioned toward the door to his partners and said to Adam, "Get off the floor, Wilson. We still have to visit your condo and we don't need you holding us up."

****

Judging by the intense pain he was experiencing every time he took a breath, Adam surmised one or more ribs on his left side were bruised or fractured. He winced when the gunman yanked him by the arm and pushed him down into a chair. Forced to sit quietly and watch while Andrakov's thugs rifled through his condominium, Adam felt the muzzle of the handgun positioned at the back of his head the entire time.

"Andrakov doesn't want this to look like a burglary," the gunman said to his partners, "so make sure the place is left in the same condition as when we got here."

Within the hour, the men had managed to take thousands of dollars in cash, cheques and jewellery.

"We're not done yet, Wilson," said the gunman, pulling Adam by his shirt out of the chair. "Let's go."

As the men exited the building the same way they entered, by the underground parking garage, the third man broke off from the group and made his way to the Hummer. With both vehicles now taken, only one luxury item remained. Adam had a sickening feeling in his gut as he presumed what was next and prayed he was wrong. His

*The Desires Of Opulence*

suspicions were confirmed when he heard the gunman say, "It looks to me like a nice night for a sail. What do ya think, Eddie?"

"Bea-u-ti-ful!" Eddie's smile was villainous.

As they walked toward the marina gate, the gunman said, "No tricks, Wilson. The three of us are going to get on that sailboat, and you're going to take us out of the marina, up the river and out on the lake without incident. Got it?"

"Ya," Adam mumbled as wave after wave of despair swept over him. It was no longer a matter of losing all of his money and material possessions to a mobster. He knew in his heart he would soon lose his life.

The marina was still, save for the waves of the Niagara River softly lapping against the breakwall and the rhythmic clanging of boat lines softly hitting the masts. It was 3:30 in the morning and not a soul was around; no one Adam could signal to, or witness his departure. When they reached the slip, all three men boarded the boat. Eddie went below deck to rummage around while Adam and the gunman remained topside. Adam managed to concentrate through the pain, and manoeuver the Hunter out of the marina and onto the Niagara River for what he knew was the last time. He frantically began to think of a way to escape. If he threw himself overboard and managed to avoid being shot, he would never make it to land. He was a strong swimmer but the injury to his ribs would greatly hinder him. There was complete silence from all three men until the boat reached the mouth of the river feeding into Lake Ontario. The June night air was warm with variable winds and waves of less than a foot in height. The moon was full and cast a runway of light upon the dark expanse of water. The lights from a freighter flickered in the distance.

Eddie appeared in the light of the cabin doorway with a bottle of Crown Royal in his hand. He took a swig before handing it up to the gunman.

"Okay, Wilson, now you're going to raise the sails and travel in a north-easterly direction. I will tell you when to cut the engine," said the gunman before taking a drink.

Adam would have given anything for some of that whisky to dull the pain and calm his fears. His greed and arrogance had gotten him into this situation and it would take a miracle to get him out of it. All he could do was try.

"Look, uh, fellas," he said, "I didn't mean to be disrespectful to Mr. Andrakov. I've been under a lot of pressure lately."

"Well, I'll tell ya something, Wilson. You've got pure shit for brains. Did you actually think Andrakov would stand idly by while you threatened to spill your guts to the cops?"

"I wasn't going to go to the police. I just said that because I was frustrated. In fact, I was going to call Mr. Andrakov and attempt to smooth things over."

"Ya, like I haven't heard that before." The gunman again raised the bottle of liquor to his lips. "So now you are no longer someone Mr. Andrakov can trust. It's as simple as that."

"Look, just call up Mr. Andrakov and tell him I'll take on as many partners as he wants," Adam pleaded. "I'll service him and the others exclusively. No bullshit, no attitude. I won't even expect a commission. Please, just call him!"

With a smirk on his face, the gunman looked over at Eddie and shook his head. "It's too late, Wilson. Like I said before, you're no longer someone Mr. Andrakov can trust. There is no second chance, and that's what shitheads like you don't get. Right, Eddie?"

Eddie was chuckling. He loved this part of his job: watching smart-asses like Wilson grovel for their lives. "Right."

The sorrow Adam felt was overwhelming as he looked up into the starry sky and struggled to fight back the tears. As he steered the boat toward the middle of the lake, he thought of his family. They would never know what happened to him; he would disappear without a trace. His mind was racing as he raised the sails. There may be a chance he could force the thugs overboard. It might be worth a shot. He just had to time it right.

Almost an hour into the sail, the Hunter was picking up speed. Both of Andrakov's men were now topside; Eddie was standing at the stern, holding on to the railing, the embers from his cigar glowing bright red in the darkness, while the gunman was seated facing the helm, his pistol still pointed at Adam.

*It's now or never.* Adam suddenly spun the wheel hard to port. As the sailboat keeled over, Eddie was thrown off balance, his massive body toppling over the railing. The gunman managed to hold on, although he was now lying flat out on the seat, arms and legs flailing. The gun flew out of his hand and skidded across the deck. Adam pounced on top of the gunman, landing two punches to the man's face. As the Hunter righted itself, both men were thrown to the deck. With every ounce of strength he had, Adam pulled the gunman off the floor and attempted to throw him over the side, but he was no match for the burly thug. Within moments he was overpowered and being held in a crushing bear hug. He yelled out in agony, the pain from the pressure on his rib cage more than he could bear. Eddie had managed to grab on to the railing, and with an extreme amount of effort, pulled himself back on board. Enraged, he descended on Adam and screamed, "You son-of-a-bitch! I'm going to fucking kill you!" He drove his fist squarely into Adam's face. As teeth and bone shattered, Adam could taste the blood and began to choke. The gunman loosened his grip as Adam slumped, then dropped to the deck floor. The pain was searing. As Eddie continued to rant, his wet boot connected with Adam's rib cage, then his stomach. Blood and saliva spewed from Adam's mouth and he writhed in pain, barely able to breath, barely able to utter a sound.

After locating the pistol, the gunman grabbed the wheel of the boat, steering it back on course. Attaching the silencer and handing the gun to Eddie, he demanded, "Plug 'em!"

Eddie got in two more kicks to Adam's head causing him to lose consciousness. He didn't hear Eddie say, "Nighty-night, tough guy," before aiming the pistol and pulling the trigger.

## Chapter Twelve

While the warm days of spring grew longer and dissolved into the sultry days of summer, Katelyn and Dan spent hours together touring Niagara by foot, bicycle and car. By the end of the week, Dan noticed the twinkle had returned to Katelyn's eyes, and she was laughing at his weak jokes and silly puns. Time was passing far too quickly for his liking. The hours spent sleeping were hours he wasn't with her. And though he wanted more than anything to remain there until she was ready to leave so they could fly back to the west coast together, he had a meeting with a major new client he couldn't miss.

The morning Dan's plane was scheduled to fly out of Hamilton, Katelyn stopped by the Moffatt Inn where they ate a light breakfast of coffee and bagels on the terrace before he checked out.

They walked to the rental vehicle and Dan placed his suit bag in the trunk. "I wish I didn't have to leave you here," he said.

Katelyn gave him a reassuring smile. "I'll finish things up as quickly as I can."

As they embraced, Dan took pleasure in the sweetness of her lilac-scented hair, and the feel of her body pressed against his. He fought the urge to kiss her, to tell her how much he loved her. Struggling to conceal his sadness, he entered the car and started the ignition. "I'll call you tonight, Kate."

As Dan drove away, he frequently glanced in the rear view mirror until he could no longer see Katelyn waving goodbye.

****

Katelyn wanted nothing more than to go home. The episode with Adam had left her shaken and on edge. Had Dan not been there to intervene, who knows how far Adam would have gone? She shuddered at the thought.

Katelyn had decided that if the house wasn't sold within the next two weeks, she was leaving Niagara anyway. The agent would have to fax any purchase offers to Neufeld, Ramcharan.

To her delight, she received a phone call mid-week from the real estate agent. There was an offer on the house and it was very close to the asking price. The potential buyers were a retired couple from Toronto who fell in love with the town during a recent visit. When the agent stopped by, Katelyn wasted little time signing the papers. A quick closing date was agreed upon by both parties, and the deal was completed. A local dealer came by to appraise and purchase the antique china, glassware, lamps and smaller pieces of furniture. The dining room and bedroom suites, and living room settee would remain with the house, as well as the window treatments and large appliances. She would take her mother's photo albums and jewellery with her on her trip back to Vancouver. All the other treasures she couldn't bear to part with would be shipped by UPS.

Katelyn spent her last evening in town with Cheryl. Her friend had just found out she was pregnant, and most of the conversation revolved around plans for the baby's arrival. Katelyn spoke very little of Adam, only to say that their weeks together were passionate and intense.

Cheryl couldn't resist asking about Dan. "So, are you going to pursue something with that delicious boss of yours when you get home?"

Katelyn groaned. "I was hoping we could get through this evening without you bringing that up!"

Laughing, Cheryl replied, "Are you kidding? Not a chance!"

Katelyn slowly shook her head, pretending to be disgusted. "Trust me, girlfriend, if anything happens, I promise you'll be the first to know."

Cheryl's expression grew serious and she said, "Katie, believe me, honey. What you and Adam experienced these past few weeks is forgettable. What is waiting for you upon your return to the west is the real deal. I don't profess to be an expert on love, but I know one thing. What I saw that afternoon outside the post office was a man deeply in love with you."

\*\*\*\*

The driver placed Katelyn's luggage in the trunk and climbed into the driver's seat. He turned back to her and smiled.

She returned the smile and said, "John Monroe Airport please. I have an 11:00 flight to Vancouver."

She took one last look at the little house before the airport limousine pulled away. Ashton was quietly nestled in his cat carrier on the seat beside her. She had visited her parents' graves early that morning, said a prayer and tearfully told them how much she loved them. A chapter of her life was now closing.

She decided against calling Adam's mother to say goodbye. Her feelings were too raw, and she didn't know what Adam had told his family about their relationship, if anything. She would thank the Wilsons for their caring and support at a later time.

Katelyn glanced down at her parents' matching gold wedding bands she had resized to fit the ring finger of her right hand. They were a beautiful token of the enduring love and commitment shared by two people. She recalled her conversation with Cheryl from the previous evening. If her friend was correct, and Dan was to play a major part in her life, she needed time. Time to work through the grief, betrayal and regret that cluttered her mind and invaded her heart. Her relationship with Dan needed to be free of all that. He deserved nothing less.

****

Katelyn's flight was due to arrive in Vancouver early that afternoon and Dan was anxious to see her again. As far as work was concerned, most of the morning had been a write-off. Unable to concentrate, he finally left the office and went to the gym. Soaked in perspiration after a gruelling two hour workout, he finished with a relaxing sauna. As his thoughts turned to Katelyn once more, he glanced down at his watch. If the plane was on time, he would be seeing her in about an hour. With her close to him again, maybe now he'd be able to settle down and refocus on the firm; nevertheless, there was one issue still unresolved. He wanted her in his personal life. Seeing her at the office was no longer good enough.

By the time Dan showered, dressed and drove to the airport, it was just before 2:00 p.m. When he spied Katelyn riding the escalator down to the baggage area, he once again felt the intoxicating effects that can only come from being in love. She was scanning the crowd in search of him, and when their eyes met, she broke out in a glorious smile. She waved to him and called out, "I just have to pick up Ashton!"

Dan waved back and nodded before she made her way to the Special Services area. Returning with her precious cargo, she set the carrier and her two pieces of luggage on a cart, and quickly made her way to where Dan was waiting.

"Welcome back, Kate," he said as she greeted him with a hug. He inhaled deeply—lilac—it was his very own aphrodisiac.

"It feels as though I've been away forever," Katelyn replied with a sigh.

Leaving the airport, Dan drove his silver Lexus down Grant McConachie Way, over the Arthur Lang Bridge and north on Granville Street in the direction of Katelyn's West Fifth Avenue residence. The rising office towers and condominiums of downtown Vancouver dwarfed in comparison to the mountains that loomed majestically in the background. The bluish-white snowcaps had disappeared, and the various shades of lush green forests rose up to meet the clouds.

"I never grow tired of this view," Katelyn commented, absently. "I remember the very first time I drove down this street. It took my breath away."

"Yes, it is stunning, isn't it?"

"God's magnificent handiwork." She paused for a moment then continued, "Dan?"

"Yes?"

"I just want to let you know how much I treasure our relationship. You will never know how much your trip to Niagara meant to me. My life felt like it was spinning completely out of control until I saw you standing at the door. You were a lifeline."

Dan could hear the quiver in her voice and reached over, placing his hand on top of hers. "Well, I knew you shouldn't be trying to work through this terrible tragedy by yourself. A person can only handle so much adversity. You mean a lot to me too, Kate." He wanted to tell her how much he hoped the relationship could evolve into something more, but knew it should be saved for another occasion. She would need time for her heart to heal. He knew the emotions involved with losing a loved one, and that time miraculously dulled the pain, eventually healing the wound.

****

"Welcome to your new home, Ashton!" Setting the pet carrier gently on the floor, Katelyn opened the door and allowed the cat time to venture out and explore on his own. He cautiously approached the opening, his gold eyes wide with wonder, his nose and whiskers twitching.

Feeling a sense of liberation, Katelyn took in the familiar airiness and casual ambience that was her home. Her taste in furnishings was very different from her mother's. She preferred a more contemporary look of overstuffed couches, chairs and ottomans in beige and chocolate leather. It was important to Katelyn that anyone who entered her home feel immediately relaxed and comfortable; their soft place to land if only for a short period of time.

Katelyn set out bowls of cat food and water for her new family addition while he investigated the large potted palms situated around the living room. She popped a frozen entrée into the microwave before taking her suitcases to the bedroom. Even though she was tired from her trip, she went about the task of unpacking. One of the last items she removed from the carry-on was the black velvet box from Adam. Katelyn delicately removed the diamond earrings and placed them in the palm of her hand. Momentarily held hostage by her own thoughts, she was immediately transported back to the one and only time she wore them. Once again, intense feelings of resentment and hurt gripped her heart. The gift she used to view as special and exquisitely beautiful was now a token of ultimate betrayal. Walking over to her desk, Katelyn removed the telephone book from the drawer and scanned the business pages for the nearest pawn shop.

****

A commotion down the hall had drawn Dan away from his desk. When he reached his office door to investigate, he saw Katelyn surrounded by Jaz and their team of people, laughing and talking. Pleased, he hung back and watched the happy reunion as she hugged each person. She was back with her extended family, her only family now. She appeared rested, the dark circles under her eyes no longer visible. As the crowd dispersed and everyone went back to their desks, Katelyn caught his gaze and returned his smile.

"I can't imagine this place without you, Kate," he said. *I can't imagine my life without you.*

"That's very sweet. Thank you."

When Katelyn arrived at her office, sitting on the corner of her desk was a delicate lead crystal vase. Inside it was a single yellow rose tipped with red. Although a card didn't accompany it, she knew who it was from. Remembering her conversation with Cheryl, Katelyn logged on to her computer and queried 'rose colours' on the Internet. To herself she read, "yellow tipped with red—the promise of love". She smiled.

Later that morning, when Dan met with his partner to go over the week's project deadlines, Jaz commented, "Everyone is so happy to have Kate back. You must be ecstatic!"

Dan nodded, getting up from his desk to pour himself a glass of water. "She is such a strong young woman, Jaz. She's been through one hell of a firestorm. I don't know that I could handle what she's had to endure these past few months."

"I know I couldn't," replied Jaz. "You know, Dan, we've discussed making Kate a partner in the firm. Why don't we offer her the opportunity now? There couldn't be a better time."

"Great idea!" Dan exclaimed. "Let's arrange to take her out to dinner in the next couple of weeks and ask her then."

"Agreed. Now, about *your* plans," Jaz said. There was a twinkle in his dark brown eyes. "Are you going to ask her out on a date, or tell her how you feel over drinks?"

Dan laughed. "Neither for now. I'm going to give her time to settle back into her life. She needs to mend emotionally. I've been without someone this long, I can wait awhile longer."

## Chapter Thirteen

Joy and Ron Wilson hadn't seen or heard from their son in over two weeks. He may have been called away on business, or decided at the last minute that his schedule was clear enough to take a few days vacation. Whatever the circumstance, it wasn't like Adam to miss spending Father's Day with the family. That's what had them concerned. Had he been forced to miss it, he would have called Ron to explain. Joy decided to drive by the marina to check and see if the sailboat was still docked. Pulling up to the gate, she was able to see his slip from the road. The Hunter wasn't there. Requesting entry from the guard, she parked her vehicle and made her way to the main office.

"Hi, can I help you?" asked the young man behind the counter.

"Yes. I'm Joy Wilson. My son, Adam, keeps his sailboat here. I was wondering if you could tell me if you have seen him around in the last week or so."

The man frowned. "Uh, let me think. The last time I saw Adam he was fuelling up." He tilted his head in the direction of the gas pumps situated directly out in front of the office. "That was, oh, two weeks ago maybe?"

"Did he mention he was going anywhere? With the boat, I mean."

"Not that I can recall. Maybe the dockmaster knows." He turned to address a slightly older man entering the office. "Did Adam Wilson tell you he was going on a sailing trip?"

The dockmaster shook his head. "No. He doesn't usually."

"You wouldn't happen to recall the last time you saw him, would you?" Joy asked.

He glanced over at the calendar hanging on the wall. "June 4th? Maybe 5th? Somewhere around then. The sailpast was taking place that weekend, and I remember Adam was stocking up the Hunter. I asked him if he was going to miss the event and he mumbled something like, 'I'm afraid so,' or 'I guess so.' I could tell he wasn't in a very good mood so I didn't say anything more."

Joy thanked the men for their help and left the office. *Damn, that kid! Why is it so hard for him to let someone know he'd be away?* She wasn't one of those doting mothers who had to know where her kids were every moment of the day, but she did insist Adam tell her when he was taking the boat on a trip and when he was planning on returning. She had heard her share of stories of boaters having problems with their sails, mechanical difficulties, or worse, falling overboard and drowning. Irritated, she dialled his cell phone number and was directed to his voicemail. "Adam, this is your mother," she said sternly. "Call us please. We just want to know if you're all right."

Over the next couple of days, whenever the telephone rang, Joy hoped it was Adam, only to be disappointed when it wasn't his voice on the other end of the line. Positive that Katelyn Ross would know where he was, if not physically in his company, Joy was surprised to discover the Ross telephone line was no longer in service. Did Katie return to British Columbia? And if she did, why wouldn't she call or drop by to say goodbye? She didn't have the young woman's cell phone number or home phone number in Vancouver. What the hell was happening? Suddenly, an intense feeling of dread washed over her, penetrating to the core of her being. Her next call was to the Niagara Regional Police.

****

When Wyatt read Adam Wilson's name on a recent list of Missing Persons, he called the officer in charge of the case, Detective Jennifer Kennedy.

"It appears you and I have a common interest in someone by the name of Adam Wilson. I'll share my information if you share yours," Wyatt joked.

"Sharing is good," Kennedy laughed. "How do you know Adam Wilson?"

"I'm investigating him for fraud. Who reported him missing?"

"His parents, Ron and Joy Wilson."

"How long has it been since they've seen him?" Wyatt asked.

"According to his mother, the last time Wilson dropped by her home was on May 30th. She remembers seeing his car parked in front of his office on the morning of June 3rd."

"Almost a month ago," Wyatt mused.

"Yep. Mrs. Wilson suspected he took his sailboat on a trip when she drove by the marina and saw it wasn't docked in the slip. She found it strange that he didn't ask her to pick up his mail as he usually does whenever he leaves town. She has left numerous messages on his cell phone, but he hasn't returned her calls. She's afraid he may have had a boating accident and drowned."

Maybe, but not likely, Wyatt thought. He had his own suspicions. "Did anyone at the marina see him leave?"

"No," replied Kennedy. "Marina staff told her they hadn't seen him since June 4th or 5th. They told me the same thing. Some of the boaters I spoke to said they saw Wilson around noon on June 5th carrying shopping bags onboard his sailboat. Apparently he wasn't in the mood for conversation; just grunted a hello and kept walking, which they say is very unusual for him. He spent a couple of hours cleaning the boat and checking the rigging and then left in his car. No one witnessed the sailboat leave the dock."

"Anything else?" Wyatt was scribbling wildly in his notebook.

"Just that the boat was christened *'Empress of the Lake'*. Bulletins have been issued to every police service and border agency throughout the country, as well as marinas along the shores of Lake Ontario, Erie, and the St. Lawrence River. That's it. Your turn."

"Okay. Wilson is a financial investment broker with his own company which I'm sure you already knew—"

"Yep. Knew that," Kennedy responded.

"The complainant, Miss Katelyn Ross, called us on June 1st alleging Wilson stole tens of thousands of dollars from her mother, who is now deceased, over the span of one year. I met with her the following day and, based on statements she provided from the investment companies, it certainly appears he has committed investment fraud. The statements differ greatly when compared to the documents Wilson provided Miss Ross's mother."

"Hmm, interesting." Kennedy liked where this was going.

"Miss Ross described him as someone who lives a luxurious lifestyle. Drives expensive cars, wears only designer clothes, high end jewellery, and likes to throw money around."

"Other people's money?"

"So it seems. Information I obtained from Equifax shows he's in debt up to his eyeballs." Wyatt quickly scanned his notes. "He leases

*The Desires Of Opulence*

a condominium on the waterfront, an office in Niagara-on-the-Lake, and his credit cards are maxed out. He also has a one hundred and twenty thousand dollar loan outstanding on the Hunter sailboat."

"Wow! Now there's a surprise!" Kennedy remarked sarcastically.

Wyatt chuckled. "Hey, the guy has to keep up appearances. So, at the moment, I'm just waiting for the warrant to search his office. I'll let you know what I find there."

"I look forward to it!" replied Kennedy.

"In the meantime," continued Wyatt, "I'll email you the contact information for Katelyn Ross. She may be able to provide something that could assist you in your case."

****

Upon arriving home from work, Joy found her husband sitting at the kitchen table with a middle-aged man dressed in a dark suit and taking notes. *What has Ron been coerced into buying now?* Setting her purse down on the counter, she greeted the two men in a dubious manner. Ron's facial expression appeared strained as he rose from his chair. "Joy, this is Detective Wyatt from the Niagara Police—"

"Adam has drowned, hasn't he?" she blurted, her eyes wide with fear.

Ron put his arm around his wife's shoulder. "No dear, no. Detective Wyatt isn't with Missing Persons. He's from the Fraud Bureau."

Joy momentarily closed her eyes and exhaled. "Thank God!" Her heart was still beating wildly as she took the officer's extended hand and frowned. "Fraud Bureau? I'm sorry, I don't understand."

"Sit down, Joy." Ron led her to one of the four Windsor chairs positioned around the table. "The detective is investigating a complaint against Adam. One of his clients is accusing him of stealing money from their accounts."

"That's utterly ridiculous!" she protested. "Adam wouldn't do something like that. Who's making these terrible accusations?"

"I'm sorry, Mrs. Wilson," Wyatt replied, "I'm not at liberty to say. I am aware of the fact that Missing Persons is investigating the disappearance of your son. Does he usually leave town without telling anyone?"

"Not for this length of time. That's what makes this situation so disconcerting, and why we felt it necessary to contact your organization, Detective." Joy wasn't sure who she was angrier with: the unknown person who accused her son of being a thief, or the police officer who was investigating this insidious complaint.

Her facetious tone didn't go unnoticed, and Wyatt sensed this woman wasn't the type to be taken in by soft words and coddling. He cut to the chase and pulled an overstuffed envelope from his inside jacket pocket. "I have a warrant here to search Adam's place of business. Does he have an assistant or someone who answers the phone? I stopped by his office earlier and there wasn't anyone there."

"He had a clerk but she quit last month. I guess he hasn't had time to hire another one."

"Do you have a key to the office?"

Joy hesitated and looked over at Ron. Catching the exchange, Wyatt quickly remarked, "Mr. and Mrs. Wilson, I have a legal right to search the premises. If you have access to it, I strongly recommend you cooperate."

Without a word, Joy got up from her seat and walked to the counter. Grabbing her purse, she unzipped a compartment, reached in and took out a key. Giving the detective a steely look, she held it up for him to see.

*The Desires Of Opulence*

Wyatt returned her gaze and asked curtly, "Do you care to come with me in my car or follow me over there?"

"We'll follow you," Ron interjected with a faint smile before his wife could respond.

Standing, the detective collected his notebook and pen, and said, "Very well. I'll meet you there."

Outside Adam's office, Joy's hands were shaking as she unlocked the door. Wyatt entered and looked around the main office while the Wilsons sat and waited in the reception area. Within minutes, two uniform police officers also arrived and joined Wyatt in the search.

****

"Miss Ross, this is Detective Jennifer Kennedy of the Niagara Regional Police Missing Persons Bureau. Detective Wyatt gave me your telephone number. If you have some time, I'd like to ask you a few questions about Adam Wilson."

"Missing Persons?" Katelyn replied. "What has Adam done now? Fled the country?" The bitterness was evident in her voice.

"Well, that's what we're trying to determine," said Kennedy. "He was last seen by his girlfriend in the early hours of June 6th."

*His girlfriend? What a snake!* Intense feelings of anger and betrayal welled up inside Katelyn once again. She could feel her blood pressure rise and struggled to keep her composure.

Detective Kennedy continued, "Can you recall the last time you saw Mr. Wilson?"

Breathing deeply, Katelyn glanced at the desk calendar as her thoughts travelled back to the first week of June. She had received the shocking telephone call from Monica Tran and contacted Detective Wyatt on June 1st; she met with the officer the following morning,

June 2nd; Dan arrived in Niagara-on-the-Lake later that day; she met with the lawyer on June 3rd, and Adam showed up at her door the next day.

"Yes, it was the morning of June 4th. He dropped by my mother's home for a few moments."

"What did the two of you discuss?"

"We discussed how displeased I was that he had taken over my mother's investment accounts for the sole purpose of siphoning them dry. I had met with Detective Wyatt and my lawyer a couple of days earlier; however, I didn't want him to know that so I kept the conversation short."

"Yes, Detective Wyatt filled me in on his investigation. Did Mr. Wilson mention where he was going upon leaving your place?"

"No, he didn't. I never saw him again after that, and I didn't expect to once he was served with the restraining order."

"What prompted you to get a restraining order?"

"He said if I spoke to the police about what I had found out, I wouldn't like the consequences. I took that as a threat."

"What day was your flight back to Vancouver?" Kennedy asked.

"June 20th. I flew out of Hamilton around 11:30 that morning."

"Well, thank you for your time, Miss Ross. I may have more questions to ask you in the coming weeks, if that's all right."

"Certainly. I'll help you any way I can."

When their phone conversation ended, Katelyn stared out the window, her chin resting in the palm of her hand. She really wasn't surprised at Adam's sudden travel plans. She wondered how his absence would affect the fraud investigation, not to mention the lawsuit she had filed against him. She looked at her watch. It was 3:30 in the afternoon and the lawyer's office would be closed. She would call Gordon Stratton first thing in the morning. She felt like such a fool. Disgusted and disillusioned, Katelyn shook her head as she turned away from the window.

"You look troubled." Dan was standing at her door, a mug of herbal tea in each hand.

"Come in and sit down," Katelyn sighed. "I just got off the phone with a detective from Niagara's Missing Persons Bureau."

"Missing Persons? Who's missing?" Dan frowned as he set the steaming cups on the desk and sat down.

"Thank you," she said gratefully, taking in the aroma of peppermint rising from the beverage. "Adam Wilson," she scoffed, shaking her head, "for over a month now. More likely he's hightailed it out of the country!"

****

Stratton knew Katelyn Ross wasn't going to like what he was about to reveal to her. "So far the reports I've received from Niagara Police aren't good. Wilson is deeply in debt. The majority of funds in his personal and business accounts were withdrawn prior to his disappearance. We can't even go after his retirement savings accounts because he doesn't own any."

"What about his condominium? Surely that's worth close to a million dollars," Katelyn asked.

"It is, but Wilson leases it," Stratton replied, doodling on his notepad. "He also leased the two luxury vehicles. The only chattels we may be able to seize are the furnishings in his office and condominium."

"Not an awful lot of assets for someone who appeared to be well off," Katelyn said, a feeling of dejection welling up inside her.

"True," said Stratton, "but it's all part of the persona. I'm sorry, Miss Ross. I wish the news could have been better. I know this must be a big disappointment for you."

Disappointment was an understatement. "What impact will his disappearance have on the case?" she asked.

"Not much. The police will continue their search for him and the fraud investigation, and we'll proceed with business as usual. Because he's not available to receive the court papers, we'll have to serve a member of his family. It wouldn't be the first time."

As Katelyn hung up the telephone, she cringed at the thought of having to directly involve the Wilsons in her suit against Adam. Yes, they were already involved to a certain point, but now they would be forced to deal with their son's mess in his absence. When everything was said and done, would her settlement award be worth the heartache and suffering left behind?

## Chapter Fourteen

Joy Wilson looked at the court documents in disbelief. It was a civil action suit against Adam, ordering the seizure of his bank accounts, investment accounts, and any and all other assets he held. The words *Katelyn Ross* and *misappropriation of funds* stood out on the page.

"Dear Lord, this can't be true," she mumbled. The longer she studied the document, the angrier she became.

Ron had appeared in the hallway eating a sandwich. "What can't be true? Who was at the door?"

"A process server. According to these papers, Adam is being sued, and you'll never guess by whom."

"Who?" he mumbled through a mouthful of food.

Frowning, Joy handed him the documents and walked over to the telephone. "Katie Ross." She picked up the receiver and dialled the long distance operator.

Ron scanned the pages and shook his head. "This is insane. Is she the reason why that detective searched Adam's office?"

"That's what I'm about to find out," Joy replied, barely able to contain her anger. "Vancouver. Katelyn Ross."

"Joy, wait until you've calmed down. You won't get anywhere ranting and raving." Although Ron was also disturbed by what was contained within the documents he was holding, he had been on the receiving end of Joy's fury more than a few times during their thirty-five years of marriage, and knew how completely irrational she could be in that frame of mind.

"I'll do no such thing, Ron. When my kids are attacked, I'm attacked." She quickly scribbled down a telephone number and disconnected the call. "What time is it in B.C.?"

"Damned if I know," Ron replied. Not wishing to be in the immediate vicinity when his wife unleashed her wrath, he turned away from her and walked back to the kitchen.

****

Katelyn sat at the restaurant table facing Dan and Jaz. They looked like two Cheshire cats.

"Okay you two. What's up?" she giggled.

Both men looked at each other and shrugged. "Oh nothing," Jaz replied. "We just wanted to take you out for dinner to welcome you back. That's all."

"That's all," said Dan.

Katelyn wasn't convinced and gave them a sideways glance.

Jaz cleared his throat. "We were quite impressed with the RiverVale Preservation presentation you were able to put together while on leave. There wasn't one aspect of the report that needed changing. You were bang on!"

Dan nodded. "Yep. Bang on."

Katelyn studied Dan's face for clues. He was definitely excited about something, but wasn't giving her anything to work with. She

*The Desires Of Opulence*

finally responded, "Well, I'm very pleased to hear that. I know how difficult it was for you to snag that account."

The server approached the table. Dan motioned him over and whispered, "Could we have a bottle of Dom Perignon please?"

"You see, that's why we value your talents and work ethic so highly. You treat each and every account like it's special and, and ..." Jaz was searching for just the right words, "and nurture it like a mother nurtures her child. Isn't that right, Dan?"

*Good God, you're laying it on a bit thick, Jaz buddy!* Dan replied, "Uh, yes, that's right."

Katelyn burst into laughter. "Okay, what is this? The Pete and Repeat Show?"

Jaz feigned dejection. "Aww, now you've hurt our feelings, Kate. Here we are, Dan and me, no, Dan and myself, uh, Dan and I—you know I can never get that right. What we are trying to tell you is that we would like you to be a partner in our firm." Jaz looked intently at Katelyn, eyebrows raised, grinning from ear to ear, his hands outstretched like he was presenting her with an invisible gift.

Dan could no longer keep from laughing. "You are pathetic. You know that, don't you?" It was more of a statement than a question.

"What? What'd I say?" Jaz also broke up with laughter.

The server arrived with the bucket of champagne, popped the cork and began to pour.

Katelyn was at a loss for words. Did Jaz say what she thought he had said? Dan looked at her with deep admiration and said, "You are an exceptional woman, Kate. *Jaz and I*," he emphasized, turning momentarily to his buddy, "would be fools not to ask you to join us. What do you say?"

Katelyn was ecstatic. She looked at both men, smiled broadly and lifted her champagne glass. "Neufeld, Ramcharan, Ross and Associates. Gentlemen, I am truly honoured."

****

Katelyn was still riding high when she returned home from spending the evening with her two new partners. The muscles in her cheeks were aching from laughing the entire night. She said a silent prayer of thanks to her parents for teaching her to be adventuresome and independent. Had she not applied for and accepted the position at the firm, she never would have met the two endearing men who contributed to making her life so much richer. Pausing to check for telephone messages, Katelyn pushed the flashing red light on the answering machine and immediately recognized the voice she heard coming from the speaker.

"Kate, this is Joy Wilson. I just received the court papers meant for Adam and I am utterly appalled by your actions. How dare you sue my son for fraud?" Katelyn closed her eyes and took a deep breath. She had dreaded the day she would have to communicate with the Ross family. "You know, I had been trying to figure out why you left without saying goodbye and now it all makes sense. All the years we've known you and treated you like our own child, and this is how you repay us? I don't know what Adam said to get you so angry. Maybe you saw him talking to another woman, God only knows, but taking him to court is despicable. He's a good man with impeccable values, and if you think we're going to stand by and allow you to ruin his life, you'd better think again. Your mother would be ashamed if she knew you were telling lies—" Katelyn turned off the machine through a blur of tears. She couldn't bear to hear anymore. She just wanted the entire ugly situation to go away. Unfortunately, she knew this wouldn't be the last time she would hear from the Wilsons.

## Chapter Fifteen

"Jennifer, it's Wyatt."

"Mike, how goes the battle?" Jennifer was sure she knew what he was calling about. "Were you able to dig up any more on Adam Wilson?"

"Oh yes. Do you have a few minutes?"

"Absolutely!"

"Well, the boxes of documents we confiscated from his office told us a great deal. First, his bank records revealed he had dealings with four banks: two in Niagara-on-the-Lake, and two in St. Catharines. The last activity on his business accounts was June 4th at which time large sums of money were withdrawn. Records also revealed the late model Hummer and Porsche he drove were leased, and neither was found in the underground garage of his condominium. I contacted the two dealerships to see if Wilson returned the vehicles and cancelled the leases. I was informed there were no records of either vehicles being returned."

"Meaning they were possibly stolen or he sold them privately. Who would buy two leased vehicles?"

"Maybe he knew a chop shop owner, or an importer who was interested in buying hot cars. He might not get much for them, but it's more than he would have received turning them in to the dealer, and if he was on the run, he wouldn't have time to find someone to take over the leases. And there's one other thing I found out about him."

"Wait, let me guess," Kennedy interjected. "He's a cokehead."

"Nope. Good guess though. He has a weakness for gambling."

"Damn! That was my second choice."

Wyatt chuckled. "You know, if I was Wilson and decided to leave town, the Hunter would be my vehicle of choice. I'd be able to live on it for months without anyone knowing my whereabouts. I could sail from one port to the next and not even have to register with a marina. I could just anchor out aways and use a dinghy to come inland for supplies. The only time I'd be taking a risk is when I needed to dock to refuel and get the waste tank pumped out."

"Not a bad set up," Kennedy remarked.

"What about you, Jennifer? Have you come up with anything new in your investigation?"

"No, not really. I spoke with Katelyn Ross—thanks again for her number—and the last time she saw Wilson was June 4th, two days after your initial interview with her. According to her, he dropped by her place, she confronted him with her suspicions and he threatened her."

"So she didn't divulge our meeting to him. Smart woman," Wyatt remarked.

"Yep. After that, she had a restraining order placed against him and she never saw him again. Oh, I have to go, Mike. I'm told I have a call on the other line from someone who recently saw Wilson's sailboat."

*The Desires Of Opulence*

Kennedy pushed the flashing white button, disconnecting her call with Wyatt and connecting her to the caller on hold. "Detective Kennedy."

"Ya, hi. I'm Alex Saunders, dockmaster for the Port Dalhousie Marina, and I saw your bulletin about the guy from Niagara-on-the-Lake and his thirty-eight foot Hunter sailboat."

"Yes," Kennedy replied. "Have you seen the man recently?"

"Not the man, but I did see the Hunter. I pulled it from the lake earlier this month."

\*\*\*\*

There was something about Detective Kennedy's appearance the dockmaster found striking. She was tall and slim and he liked how she carried herself. Her short hair was the same colour as her eyes—dark brown. Saunders guessed she was on the backside of thirty-five. She had a professional way about her, but didn't come across as unfeeling as some cops did. She was listening intently as he described the events of that particular June morning. "The guy paid me five hundred dollars cash to help him lower the mast, hoist the sailboat from the water and load it onto a trailer."

"Is five hundred dollars the usual rate for hoisting a boat?" Kennedy asked.

"No. For a boat that size it would have been around three hundred. I told him five hundred was too much but he told me to keep the extra two bills for my trouble."

"What time of the day did this take place?"

"Seven in the morning. I remember because they were waiting for me when I arrived to open the marina office. They appeared to be in a hurry, but I told them they would have to wait a few minutes until one of my employees arrived to man the office."

Detective Kennedy scribbled in her notepad while the dockmaster explained how the boat lift was used to raise and remove boats from the water.

"You said there were two men. Can you describe them?"

"Actually, there were three men, but I didn't get a look at the guy behind the wheel of the truck. The other two had dark hair and dark complexions."

"And the boat was definitely a thirty-eight foot Hunter?"

"Yes, ma'am. I know my boats, power and sail, and it was a Hunter."

"And the name on the boat?"

"Empress of the Lake."

"Anything unusual about the two men? Tattoos? Mannerisms?"

"One of the men had a split lip and bruised cheek. Looked like he had been in a fight. Neither one of them said very much—to me or to each other."

Kennedy closed her notebook and placed it in her shirt pocket. "I'd be grateful if you could take some time to attend the station and look through the mugshot catalogue."

Saunders nodded. "Sure. Just say when."

****

The Niagara Police had issued a media release informing the public of Adam's disappearance and the investigation into his alleged fraudulent activities. Upon reading the newspaper article over her morning coffee, Joy felt her blood pressure skyrocket. "Damn them! How do they get away with printing such lies?" she shouted. "We raised Adam to be a decent and responsible person. The nerve of the police to imply he's on the run. He has nothing to hide." She was suddenly struck with a thought and began to rub her temples with the tips of her fingers. "Oh, dear Lord, how will we be able to show our faces in town?"

Ron remained silent as he spread apricot jam on the whole wheat toast Joy had set down in front of him. She was once again in rant mode and any attempt to answer her questions was pointless. This was strictly a one way conversation.

Getting up from the kitchen table, Joy retreated to the sanctuary of her backyard. Climbing vines of wild roses adorned the arbour leading into the garden. Flowering shrubs were continually in bloom throughout the spring, summer and fall, and numerous fruit trees provided her with the opportunity to make jams and preserves. A koi pond with a running waterfall was situated in one corner of the yard. Sitting on the chaise lounge with her back to the house, she pulled a package of cigarettes and a lighter from her shorts pocket. She hadn't smoked in five years and a part of her felt guilty about taking up the habit once again. She knew Ron would be furious if and when he caught her in the act, but she didn't care. She needed something to take the edge off. Touching the flame to the end of the cigarette, she pulled hard and inhaled the smoke deep into her lungs, then slowly blew it back out. The only thing she cared about was Adam. Theories of his whereabouts continuously looped through her mind. She was finding it hard to get out of bed each morning and mentally prepare herself to go to work. Knowing that her family would soon be the talk of the town, she would have to seriously consider quitting her job. Taking another drag and enjoying the calming effects of the nicotine, Joy sat back and watched her daughter's calico cat, now a permanent fixture at the pond, attempt to scoop out one of the fish with its paw.

## Chapter Sixteen

For Katelyn, the partnership offer couldn't have come at a better time and she totally immersed herself in her work. Despite the disapproving looks from Dan and Jaz, she would put in longer hours at the office or take work home. It was just the diversion she needed to keep her mind from revisiting the feelings of grief, anger and betrayal that insisted on plaguing her.

One evening, after everyone else had packed up for the day and gone home, Katelyn sat in the boardroom studying a set of floor plans she had spread out on the rectangular, mahogany table. Sensing someone behind her, she turned her head in the direction of the door and saw Dan standing there. He was carrying his suitcoat over one arm, his briefcase under the other.

"Ready to call it a day?" Katelyn asked.

"Yep." Dan walked over to the table and stood next to Katelyn's chair. "What are you working on?"

"My dream home. A 2,200 square foot, one-storey ranch." She pointed to the various rooms on the plans. "At this end of the house is the master bedroom with walk-in closet and full bathroom, the guest bedroom, the den and another full bathroom. The master bedroom and living room will have sliding glass doors, both opening out to a lanai. Hot tub and sauna here. Large kitchen with walk-in pantry and

*The Desires Of Opulence*

eating area. And finally, situated at this end of the house, a two-car garage."

"Wow! I didn't know you were designing a place of your own. It's beautiful."

"Thanks. Finding the perfect piece of property to build on will take some time. Whether it has a view of the ocean or mountains or both, it'll cost a pretty penny."

"Hmm. No doubt," Dan agreed.

Katelyn tilted her head to one side as she studied the blueprints. "I'd like to have a gas fireplace built in the living room. What do you think?"

Dan set his jacket and briefcase on a chair and leaned over the table. "You'll definitely need a fireplace to cozy up to on those damp winter nights." He pointed to the wall separating the kitchen eating area from the living room. "You could have a see-through fireplace built here and enjoy it from either room."

Katelyn's shoulder touched Dan's upper arm as she also leaned in to get a better look. "I like that idea!" She looked at him and smiled. Their heads were inches apart. Dan met her gaze, and then his eyes travelled down to her mouth. He slowly moved closer until his lips met hers.

Katelyn closed her eyes and returned his kiss. Her heart was beating frantically, brought on by the sudden rush of sexual excitement, and followed just as quickly by overwhelming feelings of apprehension and anxiety. Katelyn pulled away from Dan and pushed her chair back from the table. "I—I'm sorry," she stammered as she rose to her feet.

Dan also stood, and replied, "No, Kate. I apologize for being so forward."

Dually embarrassed, the pair were momentarily at a loss for words, until Dan broke the silence and said, "I'm going to leave before I make an even bigger fool of myself." He picked up his coat and briefcase. "Good night."

"Good night," Katelyn whispered. She watched him quickly leave the boardroom and heard the main office door close a few seconds later. She sat down at the table and inhaled deeply, attempting to calm her emotions and clear her mind. When she was able to refocus, the only emotion remaining was irritation, directed not at herself, but at Dan.

\*\*\*\*

Dan cursed himself as he rode the elevator down to the parking garage. The kiss was a sudden decision, clearly without forethought, and he felt like a lovesick teenager who couldn't control his impulses.

Arriving at his car, he unlocked the doors and positioned himself in the driver's seat. He placed his key in the ignition but didn't turn it over. Instead, he stared out the windshield at the concrete wall in front of him. "You are such a moron!" he mumbled to himself. "How is Kate going to feel comfortable around you now if she thinks you're going to grab her and kiss her at any moment?" Dan hoped she didn't see it that way.

He started the Lexus and exited the garage. As he drove along Robson towards Seymour Street, he replayed the kiss and her reaction in his mind. She did respond willingly at first; that was encouraging. He could still feel the sensation of Kate's soft lips on his, and wanted more. He wanted to wake up next to her every morning for the rest of his life. He could truly make her happy if she would just give him the chance! In frustration, he hit the steering wheel with the palm of his hand. Then, like the flash of a lightening bolt, Dan was stricken with a thought, its impact sending a shudder throughout his entire body. *Did you ever stop to think that possibly she doesn't want a romantic relationship with you?*

\*\*\*\*

The Tuesday morning after the August Civic Holiday, Katelyn had just set her purse and briefcase down on the desk when the phone rang. It was Dan's assistant.

"Good morning, Seema."

"Good morning, Kate. Dan would like to see you in his office as soon as you are available."

"I'll be right there."

Katelyn smiled as she passed Seema's desk and lightly knocked on Dan's office door.

"Come in." Dan was pouring a glass of orange juice when Katelyn entered the room.

"Good morning, Dan. You wanted to see me?"

"Good morning, Kate. Close the door, if you don't mind. Would you like a glass of juice or cup of coffee?"

"No thanks. I just finished a Starbucks." She sat down across from his desk. Since the impromptu kiss, their relationship was mostly business. Katelyn's irritation passed once she came to the realization that the cards had been stacked in her favour. After all, Dan knew nothing of her affair with Adam, or her fear of committal that resulted from it. He had made his feelings clear many times prior to the kiss. Any expressions made by her proved strictly platonic. Since that evening in the boardroom, their friendship had suffered and she was working to change that.

Dan sat back in his chair and crossed his arms. "John Carrington has requested we present our proposal to him next week at the

Carrington Restorations office in Seattle, and as usual, he would like you to make the presentation."

Katelyn nodded. John Carrington was a distinguished, wealthy, older gentleman who owned many companies, and took a keen interest in the restoration of historic buildings and the preservation of the environment. He also had a soft spot for her. The father of four sons, he had repeatedly tried to link her up with his eldest, Nathan, and eventually they did date for a short period.

At the time, Dan had found enjoyment in teasing her about the relationship. "Where is prince charming taking you tonight?" he would ask with a smirk. "Paris? Or maybe the Greek Islands? I hear Mykonos is beautiful this time of year!"

Katelyn would shake her head, trying not to laugh. "You're just jealous!" she'd quip, wagging her finger at him.

"Damn right," Dan replied. "I wish I could fly on a Lear jet across the country to see a basketball game courtside, or take a race car for a spin around an oval."

Katelyn had enjoyed the jetset lifestyle: limousines, short jaunts to California for shopping trips on Rodeo Drive, concerts in Las Vegas, five star restaurants. Money was no object.

Realistically, the interests they shared were very few. Sports was one commonality, although Nathan enjoyed it from a spectator aspect, while Katelyn was athletic and liked to participate.

He was an NRA member and an avid hunter. Katelyn couldn't understand how anyone could kill an animal for recreation. He didn't have his father's concern about the environment, and felt the discussions on pollution and global warming were a lot of hype. Their political viewpoints were completely the opposite, and they butted heads on topics like the war in Iraq, healthcare and the economy. After every heated discussion, Nathan would become sulky and withdrawn. Katelyn soon grew tired of his immaturity and broke off the relationship.

She knew John would be disappointed and was concerned about how it would affect the business relationship between Neufeld, Ramcharan and Carrington Restorations, but the older Carrington seemed to be undaunted by the situation, and continued to treat her with warmth and affection. Every Christmas he would send her a beautiful bouquet of seasonal flowers accompanied by a gift certificate for a few days of pampering at one of the local resort spas.

"Just a little something to show my appreciation," he would always say when she called to thank him for his generosity.

Her thoughts returning to the present, Katelyn remarked, "That's not a problem, Dan. I'm prepared. What day did John have in mind?"

"Thursday. Mid-afternoon. I thought we could drive there, make the presentation and stay overnight instead of rushing back here. Unless you'd prefer we return the same day."

Katelyn liked the idea. "No, that's fine. We could have a nice dinner along the waterfront and take our time coming back in the morning."

Dan replied, "Good! We can take my car. I'll pick you up at your place."

Katelyn could tell by the hint of smile on his face that her response pleased him. She rose from the chair, but before leaving his office, Katelyn turned back and said, "I'm looking forward to it."

Thursday morning dawned bright and clear. Dan arrived at Katelyn's condominium just after 9:30. They would be in Seattle by noon and have lunch before the presentation at the Carrington office. Katelyn was dressed in a yellow t-shirt, white capri pants and wedge sandals. Rather than running the risk of wrinkling her business clothes during the trip, she packed them in her suitbag with the intention of changing once she checked into the hotel. Dan had the same idea and was dressed in a pair of khaki shorts, taupe golf shirt and Sperry Top-Siders. They laughed upon seeing each other.

"Great minds think alike," he said, placing her bag in the trunk.

"It's a glorious morning for a drive," Katelyn commented as she pulled the seatbelt across her chest and buckled it. As Dan took his seat behind the wheel, she couldn't help notice his muscular tanned legs, and how the sleeve bands of the golf shirt fit snugly around his biceps. Rarely had she seen him in casual attire, never in shorts, and she found it difficult to keep her eyes from wandering back over to his side of the car. As they made their way out of the city in the direction of Highway 99, she asked, "So, how's Jason getting along in Calgary?" She knew Dan's son from when he was a teenager and would spend his summers working part-time at the firm. Now a young man of twenty-one, he was studying Business at the University of Calgary.

"Really well," Dan replied with a smile. "He graduates next spring, and from the sounds of it, he's planning on staying there."

"Good for him. Does he have any job prospects lined up?"

"The accounting firm he's interning with this summer has shown interest in hiring him."

"Great! You must be so proud of him."

"More than I can say. I talk to him every week and he seems very happy. He's such an awesome kid, Kate. He's smart, caring, funny."

"Because he has excellent role models," Katelyn said.

"Well, I have to give most of the credit to my ex-wife," he replied.

"Oh, I'm sure you were a big influence in how Jason turned out."

Dan shook his head. "No, I don't think so. I was too self-absorbed, and spent so much time trying to get the firm up and running that I neglected my wife and child."

"You're too hard on yourself, Dan. You provided for your family and worked hard doing it. I'm sure you spent a great deal of time with Candace and Jason before Neufeld, Ramcharan. Besides, the qualities you see in your son are the same qualities I see in you. They're what make you such a special person."

Dan glanced over at Katelyn and smiled appreciatively. "Thank you," he said.

She replied with a shrug, "Hey, I'm only speaking the truth."

The tension between the couple dissolved, and by the time they crossed the border into the United States, the close friendship they previously shared was restored.

Katelyn loved to hear stories of Dan's childhood and cajoled him into telling one. Being from a large family, he was never without an anecdote describing the antics of the Neufeld kids growing up in Gibsons, and this morning he didn't disappoint. By the time his tale was finished, her side hurt from laughing and she was dabbing her eyes with a tissue.

Dan looked thoughtful for a moment. "I don't think I've ever asked about your childhood, Kate. What was it like for you growing up as an only child?"

Katelyn pondered the question a few moments. "Well, I think I was pretty much the centre of my parents' attention."

Dan nodded. "As was Jason, and if I remember correctly, at times that wasn't a very good thing."

Katelyn chuckled. "I'm sure my parents would have agreed with you. They did insist on making time for themselves."

"Were you ever lonely?"

"Um, yes, I suppose I was on occasion, but it isn't something that stands out in my memory, and certainly not in a bad way. I think I grew up faster than my friends who had siblings simply because I was around adults so much. Why do you ask?"

"I wonder sometimes if maybe I was selfish not wanting to have more children back then. It might have been better for Jason. Being the second oldest of six children, by the time I grew up and moved out on my own, I felt I had already raised kids. Back then, having one child was plenty for me. Now I wish I had more."

"I can understand that," Katelyn replied. "I don't think it was a selfish decision on your part. Maybe the reason Jason is doing so well out in Alberta is because of the time he spent alone while growing up. He is probably quite comfortable with himself. Like me, he learned how to be independent and responsible at an early age."

"I guess," Dan replied.

"Besides," Katelyn added, "there's still plenty of time for you to have more children."

Dan looked over and searched her eyes.

As though reading his mind, she realized he desperately needed to know where their relationship was headed and gave him a reassuring smile. She decided now was the best time to bring up the kiss. "Dan, I'd like to explain why I pulled back from your kiss that evening."

"Kate, you don't have to explain. It was an extremely presumptuous move on my part, and I had no right to place you in that awkward position."

"No, no. You deserve to know how I feel about us. You've been upfront about your feelings for quite some time and, in return, have received nothing from me."

"I appreciate that, Kate."

Katelyn hoped she could get through her explanation without losing her composure. She hated that Adam had such a hold on her emotions. "My relationship with Adam wasn't strictly business. We were lovers. We had been dating for years before I left Ontario to move out here and we hadn't seen each other since that time. When we met up again this spring, I quickly fell back in love with him, and we continued where we left off all those years ago." She sighed deeply. "So, that is why I haven't been forthcoming with my feelings towards you. It wasn't only that Adam stole from my family and betrayed that trust; he used me for his own opulent desires, for his own selfish greed. When I backed away from your kiss, I wasn't retreating from you, but from my own feelings. I just need more time."

Seeing the joy and relief on Dan's face left no doubt in her mind that she made the right decision in telling him how she felt.

****

Katelyn was familiar with the architecture of downtown Seattle and its history. Early Seattle, settled in the mid-1800's, was predominantly a logging town. At that time, buildings were affordably constructed of wood. The Great Seattle Fire took place on the afternoon of June 6, 1889, when flames broke out in a cabinet making shop and quickly spread to neighbouring businesses. The town's water supply couldn't handle the blaze, and by the following morning, twenty-five city blocks had been destroyed. Seattle residents quickly rebuilt a new downtown of stone and brick, producing beautifully historic buildings like Pioneer Square.

Her presentation focussed on the preservation of two Queen Anne style homes in the city. John Carrington and his historic restoration committee liked the concept of restoring the buildings' exteriors and interiors exactly as they were almost one hundred and twenty-five years ago. The newest in energy efficient windows and heating and cooling systems would be introduced, as well as environmentally friendly materials that were longwearing and moderately easy to maintain. Katelyn was aware the committee members, like all historians wishing to preserve precious items from the past, were concerned with how many historic buildings were being levelled by wrecking balls each year. It was cheaper to build new structures than to restore and maintain existing buildings from eras when labour was inexpensive and craftsmanship was a word held in high regard. Every time she took part in saving a historical landmark, she thought of her hometown and how its beauty taught her to care and ensure that preservation played a part in the architecture of modern day.

Later that evening, John hosted a dinner at an upscale restaurant a short distance from Katelyn and Dan's hotel. Naturally, John insisted Katelyn sit next to him while Dan sat a few seats down the table among the various philanthropists. At one point, he noticed Dan and Katelyn's eyes meet and hold, while exchanging knowing smiles. John leaned over to her and whispered, "Do I sense love in the air, my dear?"

Feeling the warmth rising in her cheeks, Katelyn looked at John and replied, "It's a definite possibility!"

John grabbed her hand and squeezed it. "I am so pleased for both of you. Kate, I love you like a daughter, and I feel compelled to give you this advice because I know you will heed it. I have known Dan for many years and he is a truly exceptional man, and you will never go wrong loving someone with his strength of character and openness of heart. The past couple of times we've all come together, I've noticed how much happier he is."

Katelyn accepted his wisdom with an appreciative smile. "The last relationship I walked away from left me feeling deeply betrayed, John. I've needed some time to be able to trust again."

*The Desires Of Opulence*

"Dan will wait for you, Kate. How do I know? I've watched him whenever he's with you, like today in the boardroom, and he doesn't stop smiling!"

Partially listening to the conversation around him, Dan watched as the twosome at the end of the table talked intensely and looked at him periodically. Katelyn had tears in her eyes, but was smiling and nodding. Carrington was animated, and looked like he was about to explode with joy. They finally hugged and Katelyn left the table. Dan's eyes followed her until she turned the corner and disappeared from view. He glanced back at Carrington with a puzzled expression as if to say, "What's going on?"

"They're happy tears, Dan. Not to worry, she'll be back!" replied Carrington.

The dinner ended just before 10:00, and instead of accepting a ride in the Carrington limousine, Kate and Dan decided to take advantage of the warm night and walk the six blocks back to the hotel.

"You gave an exceptional presentation today, Kate. Did you see how everyone in that room was transfixed on you?"

Katelyn chuckled, "Yes, I did, as a matter of fact. I was beginning to feel uncomfortable with all those pairs of eyes glued to me. I thought to myself, I hope all of these men are interested in what I am saying, but I was constantly aware of the possibility that a button or two on my blouse may have popped open!"

Dan laughed. "No, no, you looked perfect. Not a thing out of place. I'm positive they were impressed by your intellect as well as your beauty!"

"Aw, thank you. It's always comforting to have you in attendance at these things for support and to critique my performance. I know you'll be honest with me, and I would never want you and Jaz to be embarrassed because of my shortcomings."

Dan took her arm and linked it through his. "You'll never have to worry about that, Kate. Now tell me, what were you and John talking about that brought you to tears?"

Feeling slightly embarrassed over her actions, she replied, "Well, John happened to catch our eye contact and asked me if there was love in the air."

Dan laughed. "Good old John! Always vigilant. Nothing goes unnoticed where he's concerned. And what did you say?"

Before Katelyn could answer, she felt herself being propelled forward along the sidewalk, then landing hard on her left side, her face striking the concrete. She felt her breath escape her lungs with a brutal force, and for a few seconds she was unable to move. She heard a male voice say, "Give me your wallet, motherfucker."

Dan felt his arms being tightly held on either side of him. From what he was able to observe in the seconds that followed, the guy on his left was of average build and appeared to be in his early to mid-twenties. A tattoo on his neck was partially visible from under the black t-shirt he was wearing, and he reeked of marijuana.

Seeing Katelyn motionless on the sidewalk, panic rose inside Dan. "Kate!" he called as he struggled to break free.

"Hey, asshole," said the man on Dan's right, "you think you're a tough guy and can take us both on?"

He felt the muggers' hands going through his pockets and his wallet being ripped from the left inside pocket of his suit jacket.

"I got it. Let's go!" shouted the male in the black t-shirt before suddenly disappearing into the shadows.

The man on his right released Dan's arm and also took off running. Regaining his balance, Dan stepped forward to help Katelyn, who was attempting to lift her head and shoulders off the concrete. She had a horrified expression on her face and cried, "Dan, you're bleeding!"

Looking down at his chest, he saw a red stain on his white shirt quickly spreading in size. Realizing he had been stabbed, Dan's legs suddenly felt like rubber and he dropped to his knees. *Surprisingly, I hardly feel any pain*, he thought. As he began to lose consciousness, he could faintly hear Katelyn calling his name.

## Chapter Seventeen

Jennifer Kennedy was sitting at her desk eating a strawberry Twizzler and reading through a report on a missing sixteen-year-old. She hoped the girl hadn't been lured into the world of stripping and prostitution like so many other runaways. She scanned the eight-by-ten photograph. Such a beautiful young girl.

"Jennifer," the office clerk called out, "a detective from Morality is on line two."

"Thanks, Lisa." Picking up the phone and tapping the button, she announced, "Detective Kennedy."

"Jen, it's Kyle."

"Hey, Kyle! How goes it in the land of drugs, sex and gambling?"

"Let me tell ya, it's keeping us busy. I'm just on my way out, but thought you'd want to know that we seized a sailboat during a drug raid in Fort Erie two nights ago. The identification number on the vessel has been checked and traced back to one of your missing persons, Adam Wilson."

"A thirty-eight foot Hunter?" Kennedy's heart began to pound.

"You got it. We found it in a warehouse along with a few other high-end vehicles. My guess is they were going to be smuggled over the border into the U.S. at some point."

Kennedy was thrilled. "By any chance was a black Hummer and red Porsche included in the other high-end vehicles you discovered?"

The Morality detective checked his list. "Uh, let's see. Mercedes Benz E550, Mercedes Benz S550—nope, sorry. This group was all Mercedes."

"Okay. Has the boat been fingerprinted yet?"

"Yes," replied the officer, "and you'll never guess what else the forensic technician found."

"Tell me."

"Traces of blood in the teak seats and deck floor. He also found blood droplets on the boatlines, and blood spray on the helm and under the transom seats."

"No shit? We've been investigating the possibility of foul play. Was anyone arrested during the raid?"

"Two men. We nabbed them just as they were leaving the warehouse."

"Excellent. Would you be able to send me a copy of their mugshots? I have a witness who might be able to identify them."

"Sure thing. Hope it works out for you."

"Thanks, Kyle."

****

Saunders was talking on the marine radio when Kennedy entered the office.

"Captain's Choice, this is Port Dalhousie Marina, over."

A male voice came back over the airwaves. "Would you have a thirty-foot slip for two nights? Over."

"Stand by." The dockmaster greeted the detective with a smile. "I'll be right with you. Help yourself to a coffee. I just made it." He recalled her visit from a month ago, but for the moment he couldn't remember her name.

"Thanks. Don't rush," Kennedy replied as she turned around to look in the direction he was pointing. A dose of caffeine was what she needed right about now.

Saunders momentarily studied the large wall map of the marina before resuming his conversation on the radio. "Captain's Choice, this is Port Dalhousie Marina. There is a slip available. B dock, fifty-four. Bravo five four. Over."

"Roger that, Port Dalhousie."

The dockmaster made a note of the boat name and slip number before walking around to the front of the counter to address the detective. "I'm sorry, officer, your name escapes me."

"Detective Jennifer Kennedy."

"Oh, yes, Detective Kennedy. We're hosting a salmon fishing derby this week so we're a tad busier than usual. How can I help you?" He had been reading the articles in the newspaper regarding the missing investment broker from Niagara-on-the-Lake and presumed she was back to ask a few more questions. He had visited the police station in an attempt to identify the two men he assisted that early June morning from photographs, but none of the mugshots matched.

Kennedy took a sip from the styrofoam cup before setting it down on the counter and reaching into her pocket for the documents. Unfolding the papers, she handed them to the dockmaster. "I have two new photographs to show you. Were these the two men who paid you to haul the Hunter from the water on the morning of June 6th?"

Briefly scanning the pictures, he handed them back to the detective and shook his head. "No ma'am. They're too young. If I remember correctly, the two guys I spoke with were older. In their early to mid-forties. The driver of the flatbed truck may have been one of these young guys. As I said before, I never got a look at him."

Kennedy nodded that she understood. At that moment, a couple entered the office wishing to pay their bill before setting sail back to their home port. "Well, I won't take up any more of your time. Thank you for your assistance, and for the coffee."

"If you have any other questions, I'll be here!" Saunders bid her goodbye.

Halfway to her car, Kennedy's cell phone rang. It was the forensic technician. The testing was conclusive; the blood extracted from the Hunter sailboat belonged to Adam Wilson. The detective closed her phone and looked out past the green and white lighthouse to the expanse of water.

****

Kennedy pulled up to the Wilson home and quickly made her way to the front door. She knew she would have to choose her words carefully when speaking to them.

"Detective, please come in." Ron escorted the officer to the living room where Kennedy took a seat on the couch. "I won't offer you a beer," he said, holding up the can in his hand, "but can I get you a soft drink or coffee?"

"No, thank you, Mr. Wilson. How have you and your family been getting along?" She knew the question was rhetorical. How would anyone fare knowing their child had vanished without a trace while being implicated in a crime?

Ron sat down in his recliner across from her. "Oh, we're managing as best we can under the circumstances. Do you have any further information on Adam's disappearance?"

"Well, yes, I do. Is Mrs. Wilson home?"

"She's upstairs resting. I'd rather not disturb her."

"All right." Kennedy opened her notebook and flipped to a page before continuing. "Mr. Wilson, Adam's boat was located at a warehouse in Fort Erie. The identification number is a match. We believe the people responsible for stealing it were planning to smuggle it across the border into the United States."

Ron was thoughtful and hesitated before responding. "So, the hope of Adam sailing somewhere in the Caribbean is now dashed."

"Our Forensic Identification Bureau brushed it for fingerprints and found many belonging to Adam. They also found traces of blood that tests revealed also belonged to Adam."

Ron looked intently at the officer. "So you have reason to think he may be dead?" His voice was almost a whisper.

Kennedy could see the strain on his face; Ron had aged years in a matter of weeks. Remaining composed, she calmly replied, "We don't know what has happened to your son, Mr. Wilson. Two men were arrested at the warehouse and may be able to provide us with information. The blood may have been there before Adam's disappearance. Maybe he injured himself checking the lines or during a sail. Possibly the boat being stolen at the same time Adam disappeared is simply a coincidence."

Ron bit his lower lip and nodded. Kennedy didn't think her words had an impact. She closed her notebook and rose to leave. "Please believe me, Mr. Wilson, when I say that I understand what your family is going through," she added. "I have assisted many parents in attempting to locate their children, and continuing to believe Adam is alive and well is the best thing you can do right now."

"Do you think he's alive and well, Detective Kennedy?"

She smiled reassuringly. "There is always hope. People leave their lives behind for many reasons: for a break from too many pressures, or because they're suffering from a mental illness, or—"

"Or because they've committed a crime and are running from the police," Ron interrupted. His expression was grim. "We overindulged that boy his entire life, and now we're paying the price."

## Chapter Eighteen

"Your husband is going to be fine, ma'am," the emergency doctor announced as Katelyn was having her wrist wrapped by a nurse. She made no attempt to correct him. "It's a good thing he is in such excellent physical shape. The knife blade penetrated the deltoid muscle in his shoulder and the pectoral muscle in his chest. There wasn't any damage to the lung. We've given him a tetanus shot, as well as a shot of Demerol for the pain. The stitches can be removed in about ten days. I've given him a prescription for codeine that you'll need to have filled before leaving the country. The police are asking him questions at the moment. After that, he can sign the discharge papers and you can be on your way."

Katelyn thanked the doctor before he left the room and hurried off down the hall. The nurse escorted her to the examination room where Dan was resting and talking to the two Seattle police officers. Katelyn had spoken with them earlier, but was unable to give them any type of description of the two muggers. By the time she was able to catch her breath and partially raise herself off of the sidewalk, the men were gone. She had been panic stricken at the sight of Dan bleeding from his wounds and collapsing to the ground, all the colour drained from his face. Accompanying him in the ambulance to the hospital, she held his hand the entire way and prayed he wouldn't die. She couldn't bear it if he left her.

*The Desires Of Opulence*

The relief and joy of seeing Dan sitting up in the bed, the colour now returned to his handsome face, was overwhelming. He was hooked up to an I.V., and his arm was in a sling to immobilize the shoulder. *Your prayer has been answered*, she heard her inner voice say. *Let your guard down. No more running away from the truth.*

"Hello, Sunshine." Dan smiled broadly as he held out his left hand toward her. "It was driving me crazy not being able to see you. Are you all right?"

Fighting back tears, Katelyn grabbed his hand. "I'm fine, Dan." She held up her bandaged hand and pointed to the side of her face. "Just a sprained wrist and a few scrapes. Nothing major."

She sat down in a chair beside the hospital bed, never letting go of his hand. Before leaving, the police assured the couple they would be in touch if there were any developments in the case. Whether the robbers were caught or not wasn't important to Katelyn at that particular moment.

Smiling weakly, she looked at the bandages on Dan's chest and shoulder. "The doctor said if you weren't so buff the prognosis could have been much worse. How's the pain?" *You stupid little ninny, what is wrong with you? Tell him!*

Dan replied, "The Demerol is starting to kick in. Seeing you makes everything better."

She brought his hand up to her face and looked deep into his eyes. Oh, those gorgeous blue eyes. She could gaze into them all day long. *You know he loves you, and you know he would never hurt you. You must tell him now!* Katelyn's eyes filled with tears as she tried to speak from her heart. The huge lump in her throat was making it difficult.

Wiping her tears, Dan tried to console her. "It's over, Sweetie. We're safe now and everything will be fine."

Katelyn nodded and sniffled, "Yes, thank God. I was so afraid I was going to lose you." She swallowed hard and continued, "Dan, I want to tell you something I should have told you a very long time ago." She guided his hand to her heart and pressed it against her breast. "I love you!"

****

Feeling the effects of the pain medication, Dan slept most of the trip back to Vancouver. He didn't argue when Katelyn insisted he stay with her for a few days while he recuperated. By the time she drove his Lexus into the parking lot, he was feeling weak and lightheaded. Once inside her condominium unit, she helped him get undressed and situated in a comfortable position in her bed. The cool cotton sheets felt good against his skin. Sitting next to him, Katelyn applied a cool cloth to his forehead and gently stroked his hair. Within minutes, Dan's eyes grew heavy and the last thing he remembered was feeling her soft lips against his, and hearing her sweet voice whisper, "Sleep well."

Katelyn called Jaz and filled him in on what took place in Seattle, and told him that Dan would be staying with her for awhile. He offered to stop by Dan's home, pack a few days worth of clothing and bring them to her place. When the call ended, she stepped out to get bandages and antiseptic at the local pharmacy, pick up a few items at the supermarket for dinner, and bring the luggage in from Dan's car. Dan was still asleep when Jaz dropped off the clothing. He spent a few moments chatting with Katelyn before going on his way. "Tell Dan I'll come back in a couple of days for a visit."

By late afternoon, Dan emerged from the bedroom wearing his robe and looking groggy. He ran his fingers through his tossled hair. "Something smells good. What's cookin', good lookin'?"

Katelyn giggled. "Food we don't have to cut with a knife! For starters, carrot and herb soup, followed by grilled salmon with artichoke pasta salad, and strawberry sorbet for dessert. It should be ready in about ten minutes," she said as she brushed the salmon filets with olive oil and dill.

"Sounds wonderful," he said, kissing Katelyn on her forehead. "I'll go get dressed and try to make myself presentable."

"Presentable? You look pretty good to me. No need to change. How's the pain?"

"Easing off. I took a dose the moment I got up."

"Good. Please make yourself at home here, Dan. Help yourself to anything in the fridge, pantry, medicine cabinet, whatever." As she stirred the pasta salad, Katelyn continued, "I spoke to Jaz earlier. He stopped by your place and brought over a few days supply of clothes. They're hanging in my closet. He'll come back in a couple of days to see you."

"Sounds like a good plan." Dan scanned the living room. "You've redecorated since the last time I was here. It looks really nice."

"Thanks. My gosh, yes, it's been two years since I hosted the New Year's Eve party. I remodelled the following spring."

Dan carefully sat down on the sofa, and was quickly joined by Ashton. "Hey, here's my buddy! Where've you been?" Meowing in response, the large, amiable tomcat stepped into Dan's lap and sat down.

Katelyn shook her head in mock irritation. "He's wanted to visit you all afternoon but I insisted he stay out here and let you sleep. Shoo him away if he's too pesky."

"Poor Ash, she's a mean mommy, eh? Are you going to have some salmon?" Ashton continued to meow and purr as Dan stroked his head. Katelyn laughed as she watched the two interact.

Realizing they had eaten very little since the previous evening, the couple quickly devoured the light supper. After dessert they moved to the living room to watch television. Dan reclined on the couch, his head resting on a pillow in Katelyn's lap. Feeling the relaxing effects of her touch as she stroked his hair, Dan eventually fell asleep. She looked down at him dozing peacefully. She had always loved him as a friend but she knew positively it was deeper than that the day she saw him standing on the Ross front porch. Now it was time to show him; to give herself to him completely. No more fear of betrayal. No more barriers. Cheryl was right. This was the real deal. She owed her best friend a phone call.

\*\*\*\*

Dan awoke to the sound of the rain softly tapping on the window. Although the room was partially lit, he was able to make out 7:30 on his wrist watch. He felt exhausted. He vaguely remembered Kate helping him from the living room couch to her bed at some time during the evening. He had been awakened numerous times throughout the night, the slightest movement causing pain to shoot up his shoulder and neck. He finally resorted to taking two pain pills and was able to fall back to sleep only to be jolted awake by a nightmare. In the dream he was being chased tirelessly by two men with swords. He was unfamiliar with the dark and eerie surroundings, running down street after street in search of a safe haven. Everywhere he hid, the cloaked and faceless hunters were able to find him. After what seemed like hours of running, they finally cornered him and were seconds away from running him through when he awoke breathless and perspiring, his heart pounding in his chest.

Scanning the room with his eyes only, he noticed the cat curled up in a chair in the corner. Hearing soft, rhythmic breathing beside him, Dan turned his head to see Katelyn sleeping next to him. She was lying on her side facing him, her countenance peaceful, hair strewn about her pillow. Her bandaged cheek was swollen. His panic subsided at the sight of her.

As he watched her sleep, he thought of the other night in the Seattle hospital. He had been deeply moved by her declaration of love for him. The look in her eyes and the expression on her face was pure love. As she clutched his hand and held it to her breast, he could feel her heart pounding. What he was hoping for and dreaming of all these months had finally come to pass. A feeling of contentment had washed over him, and he welcomed Katelyn's kiss as she tenderly touched her lips to his.

She was as beautiful in slumber as she was awake and he reached out to delicately move a strand of hair away from her injury. Katelyn stirred, shifted onto her back and stretched, the sheet falling away from her shoulders to expose the thin straps and plunging neckline of her nightgown. Dan felt an intense sexual yearning, and wanted more than anything to reach out and pull her to him. *I'm finally sharing a bed with this goddess, and I can't even hold her in my arms.*

"How are you feeling?" Kate was awake and smiling broadly.

"Pretty sore and tired."

"Stiff too, I'll bet. It must be difficult not being able to move freely." She got up and walked over to Dan's side of the bed. He noticed how the garment clung to her slender body as she moved, her breasts pressing against the bodice, the shadow of her pubic mound faintly showing through the delicate fabric. She kissed him warmly before helping him into the sitting position and swinging his legs over the side of the bed.

With Katelyn standing directly in front of him, Dan placed his index finger under her chin and said, "You're going to need some ice for your cheek, my love. It's quite swollen."

"I must be quite a sight," Katelyn said, gingerly touching her face.

"On the contrary. You look beautiful," Dan murmured as he rested his face between her breasts and placed his free hand on her bottom.

The touch of his hand sent a sensation throughout Katelyn's body that gave her goose bumps. She felt the soft tickle of his eyelashes brushing against her skin. She ran her fingers through his hair and down the nape of his neck. "I think what we both need is an entire day of bed rest. Why don't I make breakfast for starters, and then we'll go from there."

"Mmm, I definitely like the sound of that. God, Kate, you feel so good. I can't wait until I'm able to put both of my arms around you." Dan wasn't in a hurry to let her go.

Katelyn replied, "This feels pretty amazing for the time being." Her excitement was building. Their relationship was about to change, and she wanted to thoroughly enjoy every second of the experience.

Dan could feel her heart beating quickly; her chest was heaving. He knew she was ready to give herself to him. He moved his hand from her buttock to her shoulder and slid the strap of her nightgown down her arm, watching the soft material fall, exposing one breast. Cupping it in his hand, he rubbed his cheek against Katelyn's skin before covering her nipple with his mouth. She felt the sexual excitement flow through her body and come to rest in her belly. Dan's lips and tongue were tantalizing, and she quickly slid the other strap over her shoulder. Now naked from the waist up, Dan kissed and fondled her as she relished every stroke. When his hand travelled down her belly and inside her nightgown, Katelyn pushed the garment over her hips, feeling it settle on the floor at her feet.

Dan paused to look down at her nakedness. "You are exquisite," he said. Tenderly he touched the large black bruise that spanned her mid-thigh to her hip. He looked up at her with concern and said, "My poor angel. Does it hurt?"

She shook her head. "Not much. Not to worry."

Dan's kisses were tender as his lips travelled from her mouth, down her neck, to her bosom where he resumed snuggling. Gently rocking him, Katelyn closed her eyes and rested her uninjured cheek on the top of his head. She could have stayed in the moment forever.

"I have wanted to be this close to you for such a long time," Dan said.

"I love that you waited for me," she whispered.

"I would have waited forever," he replied. Dan's fingers began to explore her, caressing the softness of her inner thighs until they found the warm, wet place between her legs and gently made their way inside her. She closed her eyes, tilted her head back and whispered his name. His lips found their way to her nipple, and he suckled her like a baby seeking nourishment.

Katelyn softly moaned as the sweetness of rapture enveloped her. Dan felt her thighs gently squeeze around his hand. Her moans were soon replaced with a sigh of utter contentment.

****

"Kate, would you be able to help me, Sweetheart?"

Katelyn left the breakfast dishes she had been loading into the dishwasher and followed Dan's voice to the bathroom, where he was standing naked in front of the shower with his back to her. His body was spectacular. His buttocks were tight, and his back and shoulder muscles rippled. "How's it going, Adonis?"

He chuckled. "I'd like to take a shower, but keeping these sutures dry is going to be a challenge with only one arm functioning."

"Well, why don't I get in the shower with you?" she asked as she unwrapped the tension bandage from her wrist. "I'll lather you up and use the handheld nozzle to rinse you off."

Dan smiled wickedly and replied, "What an absolutely splendid idea!"

He watched Katelyn remove her clothing, instantly aroused at the sight of her body. She retrieved a tube of bath gel from the pantry and joined him in the shower.

Dan kissed her softly, laying tiny kisses on the corners of her mouth, on the tip of her nose, on her ear, and then back again to her lips. Katelyn loved his tenderness and gentle touch. After wetting his skin with the nozzle, the beads of water running down over his muscular form, Katelyn poured gel into her palm and began rubbing it into a lather. Cautiously bending down, the twinge in her hip a reminder of her own injury, her hands eagerly began their journey, starting with his feet and slowly moving up and around his rock hard calves and thighs. When she reached his groin, Dan moaned as her fingers gently lathered between his legs before wrapping around his erection. Stroking him, her hands lingered there a few moments acknowledging the pleasure he was experiencing before continuing up to his belly, her fingertips moving in tiny, soapy circles along the ripples of his six pack. "You're body is magnificent, my love," Katelyn remarked while applying more gel to her hands.

Dan looked down at her and smiled. "It's all yours, Kate. Anytime, anywhere."

She giggled and kissed his belly before reaching around to the small of his back, his hardness pressing against her chest. She lathered Dan's back as high as her hands could reach, then travelled back down to his tail bone and into the crease of his buttocks. As Dan's breathing quickened and he groaned with pleasure, Katelyn knew she would no doubt have to revisit this spot whenever they came together as one.

Lathering and massaging his buttocks a few seconds, she then made her way around to the front to resume stroking his erection. She remained there until he erupted in unbridled ecstasy.

After rinsing the soap from Dan's body, Katelyn stepped out of the shower and donned her terry bathrobe. Unfolding a large bath sheet, she wrapped Dan in it and helped him from the stall. Gently patting his skin dry, she said, "Once we return to bed, I'll change your bandages. Then we'll see how you feel after that. You might be ready for a nap."

"You are one hell of a nurse," he remarked. "I'm getting such good care, I won't want to leave here."

Katelyn kissed him softly before replying, "Then by all means stay."

****

"I promised you'd be the first one to know when my relationship with Dan went beyond friendship. We are now lovers. Consider yourself so advised."

Cheryl let out a squeal. "That's awesome, girlfriend! So how did it come about? Out with the details."

Katelyn brought her friend up to speed on the events that took place during the Seattle business trip.

"Katie, that's a terrible story." Cheryl sounded dejected.

"I can attempt to create a happier story for you if it'll make you feel better, Cher," she replied sarcastically, with a laugh.

"No, no, that's okay. So how are you both doing?"

"I'm totally fine. Just bruised. Dan's healing day by day. At the moment he's resting."

"Well, I'm really happy for you. No one deserves it more than you."

"Thanks. How's everything with you?"

"Good. I'm getting fatter by the hour, but what can you do? The kids keep asking me when their sister is coming. It's like being in the car with them and they keep asking if we're there yet. Very annoying. Hey, there's been a lot of drama going on around here lately."

"Oh ya? What kind of drama?"

"Well, for starters, the police are investigating Adam Wilson for fraud. Can you believe that?"

Katelyn hesitated, debating whether or not to reveal what she knew to her friend. Unaware of how far along the police were in the case, she didn't want to hinder the investigation by discussing it with anyone other than Dan and her lawyer until she was given the go-ahead. She loved her friend dearly; nevertheless, Cheryl was a chatterbox, and a story like this would be too hard to keep to herself. Feeling it wasn't the right time, Katelyn decided against it. She simply said, "Hard to believe. The town must be buzzing."

"Like bees whose hive has just been invaded by a black bear. There was a media release from Niagara Police informing the public of his fraudulent activities, and requesting anyone who might be a victim to come forward. And to make matters worse, he's off the grid; his whereabouts are unknown. The rumours are that he's skipped town and is evading authorities."

Katelyn felt her hair being lifted and Dan's lips brushing her left ear. She closed her eyes and tilted her head to the right side as a tingle travelled down her spine. "Sounds like quite the mystery. Uh, Cheryl, I have to go, hon. Dan needs me. I'll call you soon." Ending the call and setting her iPhone down, she turned to face her lover with a smile. She placed her hand on his cheek and looked into his eyes.

"You don't know how much I need you," he said before pressing his lips against hers.

## Chapter Nineteen

The salmon and lake trout were running deep. It was a scorching late August afternoon, and one of the three fishermen out trolling had already caught a Chinook an hour into the trip. A twenty pounder he guessed, maybe twenty-five. The 30-foot Grady-White slowly made its way across the lake, the counter on the downriggers was showing a lure depth of one hundred and thirty feet.

"That's one hellava Chinook you got there, Pooch," remarked one of the men. "I hope there's another one that size or better out here with my name on it."

"See, Red, I told you the new flasher would make a difference."

"Bullshit!" snorted the third man. "It's the type of bait you used."

"Like hell!" retorted Pooch. "The pros say that flasher is one of the best on the market."

"Jesus, here we go again!" said Red, directing his disgust to the third man. "You had to stir it up, didn't you, Mark? Just once I would like to go an entire fishing trip without the two of you—"

Red's rant was interrupted by the sound of all three downrigger releases popping open simultaneously. The three men stared at the equipment in disbelief.

"What the hell? Three fish biting at once? Not a chance," said Pooch.

Taking the rods from their holders, they proceeded to reel in.

"Mine's not putting up much of a fight," said Mark, checking his buddies' rods before looking back at his own.

"Neither is mine," added Red, "but there is definitely something on the end of this line."

The mysterious object was gradually making its way to the surface of the water.

"Jesus, what is that?"

"Beats the hell out of me. Keep reeling."

"Looks like something wrapped in a blanket." Pooch placed his rod back in the holder and called to the captain, "Al, cut the engines." With the outboard motors silenced, the boat bobbed in the swells as Pooch pulled the bundle closer to the side with the grappling hook. In an instant, curiosity gave way to horror as the men realized what they had snagged. The stench was overpowering.

"Holy fuck!" screamed Mark as he dropped his rod and jumped back. He collided with Pooch who was also trying to distance himself from the grisly discovery. Mark managed to make it to the opposite side of the boat before vomitting into the water. Red, also overcome by nausea, dropped to his knees on the deck.

As the rancid odour permeated the entire boat, Al covered his nose and mouth with his hand. While the smell of rotting fish and venison no longer phased him, this was something completely different. Turning to face the stern, he looked questioningly at his friends. Mark continued to throw up, while Red sat on the deck floor, his head in his hands.

*The Desires Of Opulence*

"It's a fucking dead body," Pooch croaked, refusing to look back over the transom.

As though the appearance and actions of the men weren't enough to convince him, the captain took three steps to the back of the boat and leaned over the side. Retching, he stumbled back to the helm, grabbed the radio and turned the dial to channel sixteen. "Mayday, mayday, mayday. This is Al's Party. Over."

Almost immediately, a voice came back. "Al's Party, this is Prescott Coast Guard. Over."

"Ya, uh, Coast Guard, we request assistance. Over." It took everything in his power to keep from vomitting.

"Al's Party, what is the nature of your emergency? Over."

Al attempted to clear the bile from his throat. No matter how many times he swallowed, it continued to burn. "We've discovered a body."

After a few seconds of silence, "Al's Party, please repeat."

*Jesus, is he deaf?* Al spoke slowly and deliberately, "We've hooked a body, Coast Guard! Over."

"What are your coordinates? Over."

The captain looked down at his global positioning system and read the coordinates back to the dispatcher. "We're approximately seven nautical miles from Port Dalhousie," he added.

"We'll send assistance immediately," replied the Coast Guard dispatcher.

"Al's Party, this is the Niagara Police Marine Unit. We copy that, and will be at your location shortly. Over."

\*\*\*\*

Sergeant Pierre Gaston spotted two men standing on the bow of the fishing boat waving their arms. Thirty minutes had lapsed from the time he intercepted the mayday call to the time he and his crew of three constables pulled up alongside the Grady-White. A handful of boats, manned by the morbidly curious, had also heard the distress call, and were circling around the site with hopes of catching a glimpse of the discovery. The offensive odour prevented them from venturing too close. Boarding the fishing boat from the port side, two of the constables proceeded to take statements from the sickened and extremely shaken men, while Sergeant Gaston and the third constable slowly motored around to the starboard side, tied the vessels together, and tended to the corpse. The remains had been wrapped in a blanket or bedspread, now black from mould, and strapped with nylon dock lines and black electrical cord. Gaston noticed one end of the cord was frayed. Exposed from the shoulders up, the corpse was unrecognizable; its remaining flesh looked similar to slime and was a putrefied colour of greenish-black.

"Don't you just love these old recoveries," remarked the constable, pulling a jar of Vicks VapoRub from the first aid kit and applying a dab under his nostrils.

"They're the best," the sergeant replied. He inspected a gaping hole where the nose and left eye used to be. "The fish were obviously hungry."

To prevent the body from sinking once it was cut free from the fishing lines, the officers tied a thick cord to one of the algae-covered ropes used to secure the blanket in place. Once the corpse was secure, Gaston began to videotape the scene while the constable took notes.

Careful not to disturb evidence, Gaston gingerly lifted back the blanket to expose an anchor. "Look, it's been weighted down. And judging by this electrical cord here, there may have been a heavy appliance also strapped on."

*The Desires Of Opulence*

The constable leaned in to get a closer look. "A generator, perhaps?"

"Perhaps. See the exposed wires? It looks like the cord has been chewed through. Obviously someone didn't want the body found, and it would probably still be at the bottom of the lake had these men not hooked it."

"Want me to contact Ident and Homicide?" asked the constable as he stood upright, removed his police issued ball cap and wiped the perspiration from his brow.

"Ya, and we'll need division officers to cordon off the Port Dalhousie pier before we bring the body back to land. The coroner will also have to be notified."

Waiting to be interviewed and watching from the bow of the fishing boat, Pooch called out to the officers, "I don't know how you guys can stand to be that close, let alone touch it!" He continued to hold his nose while shaking his head in disgust.

"You get used to it," the sergeant replied nonchalantly, pulling an orange perforated body bag from one of the storage compartments. He and his team had spent hundreds of hours patrolling the Niagara waters of Lake Ontario, Lake Erie, and the Welland Canal; search and recovery was a part of their mandate. They were also required to assist the Niagara Parks Police in recovering bodies from the Niagara Gorge located at the bottom of Niagara Falls, an extremely dangerous undertaking. Every year, numerous suicides took place at the Horseshoe Falls, and surviving the plunge was extremely rare. Drowning was only one cause of death. A body surfacing from the eighteen-hundred foot drop wasn't a pretty sight. The force of the water pounding on the rocks below was enough to rip limbs from bodies and crush skulls.

"How long do ya think it was under the water?" Pooch prodded.

The sergeant shrugged, "It's hard to tell. The water would be awfully cold at this depth, and it would slow down decomposition. My guess is a month, maybe two."

Gaston was joined onboard by one of the interviewing officers. "Want me to put on a wetsuit and help lift it from the water?"

Gaston shook his head. "No. Seeing that it's already somewhat bundled, I think the three of us can lift it out from here. Help me position the bag around the body before we hoist it out with the basket."

Moving the remains onto its side, Gaston noticed a hole in the back of the skull. "Check this out. Looks like a bullet wound," he said, reaching for the videocamera.

"Yep, sure does," agreed the officer, "which makes you wonder what other wounds are beneath this blanket."

With the corpse bagged and strapped into the recovery basket, it was then lifted from the water and set down on the deck of the police boat.

While the remaining interviewing constable was wrapping up, the third constable received a call on his cell phone. "Sergeant, everyone's been notified," he advised. "They'll be waiting for us at the pier."

****

Wyatt detected a note of urgency in Jennifer Kennedy's voice.

"Jennifer, how are things?"

"Ever-changing, Mike. Listen. I presume you heard about the three fishermen who reeled in a body over the weekend."

"I did."

"Well, according to dental records, it was Adam Wilson. The autopsy revealed he sustained a gunshot wound to the head."

"Bullistics?"

"Twenty-two calibre."

"Aha. No exit wound. The bullet enters the skull and fragments as it rattles around inside the brain."

"Uh-huh. And a bullet exiting the body and penetrating a boat could be disastrous."

"Jesus, I don't suppose he was looking too pretty with the fish nibbling on him all this time. You gotta feel for the fishermen who discovered him. Not quite the catch they were expecting."

"Yes, it's unfortunate. Wilson also had three broken ribs and a fractured cheekbone, possible indicators he was beaten before the murder. The Port Dalhousie dockmaster mentioned one of the men who hauled out the Hunter had a split lip and bruised face. My guess is Wilson put up a fight before he bought it."

"Makes sense," Wyatt agreed. "What about the culprits they arrested at the time of the raid? Did they recognize Wilson's photo?"

"They swear they don't know a thing about him or his disappearance," Kennedy replied.

"Do you believe them?"

"Ya. They claim they were ordered to the warehouse by someone named Eddie, and the boat and vehicles were already in storage when they arrived. Morality is looking into it. Anyway, the toxicology tests will take a few days. I'll let you know the results when I get them." Kennedy sighed. "I now have the extremely unpleasant task of informing that poor family their son was murdered."

## Chapter Twenty

"Is your husband home?" Detective Kennedy was standing at the Wilson front door with a man Joy had never met before. He was short and stocky, with gray eyes and shaved head. She presumed he was another plainclothes officer.

"Ron, we have company!" she called out in the direction of the kitchen. "He's fixing a clog in the sink," she informed her guests. Joy noticed their expressions were sombre and was beginning to wish she hadn't answered the door.

Kennedy waited until Ron joined them before introducing her partner. "This is Detective Ken Haines. Would it be all right if we sat down?"

"Yes, of course. Please excuse my manners," Joy replied. "Can I get you something cool to drink?"

The officers declined the offer. "Mr. and Mrs. Ross, Detective Haines is from the Homicide Bureau. I'm not sure if you're aware of the body retrieved from the lake near Port Dalhousie this past Sunday."

"Uh, yes, we heard about it on the news," Ron replied, swallowing hard. He studied both officers, his eyes wide with panic. "You're here to tell us it's Adam, aren't you?"

Detective Haines cleared his throat. "Yes, we're very sorry. His body has been positively identified."

Joy vehemently shook her head. "I don't believe it! That's absolutely insane!" She looked at Kennedy who was sitting beside her, and demanded, "I want to see the body for myself."

Kennedy reached out and touched her hand. "I'm sorry, Mrs. Wilson, that's not possible."

"Why not?"

"Adam's remains could only be identified by dental records and DNA."

"Because he had been in the water for such a long time," Ron interjected. He had tears in his eyes.

"Yes," she replied softly, casting her eyes to the floor.

Joy refused to believe a word they were saying. "Well, you're wrong! As I told you before, he's sailing in the Caribbean." She caught Kennedy's glance in the direction of her husband. He was shaking his head. "What? Tell me!" she demanded.

"Mrs. Wilson, Adam's sailboat was located by Morality officers in a warehouse near Fort Erie," Kennedy advised.

"And how do you know the boat was Adam's?" Joy asked hotly.

"Blood evidence found on the boat belonged to Adam." Haines leaned forward in his chair before continuing. "The autopsy revealed your son was murdered. He sustained a gunshot wound to his head."

"Oh, dear Lord!" groaned Ron, closing his eyes tightly.

"Don't tell me anymore!" Joy yelled as she sprung to her feet and pressed the palms of her hands against her ears. "I don't believe it!"

"Joy, calm down," warned Ron, jumping from his chair and rushing over to his wife.

Pushing him away, she shouted, "I won't calm down, damn it! I've had my fill of the police. First of all, that smug son-of-a-bitch from the Fraud Department accuses my son of stealing from people, and demands we hand over evidence to frame Adam with—"

"Joy, stop, please!" Ron cried.

"Now, they're saying Adam's dead—without showing us—any proof. Who—in God's name—would want to kill our boy?" She was losing her breath, and she thought her heart would explode inside her chest.

"Mrs. Wilson, are you all right?" Kennedy asked.

Joy had never felt such anger. She pointed to the door. "Get out—of my house—" The room began to spin. She took two steps forward before crumpling to the floor.

****

Joy awoke feeling groggy. Looking around she realized she was in a hospital examination room. *What am I doing here?* She could hear voices in the hall directly outside; one belonged to her husband, the other was unrecognizable. When Ron entered the room, she greeted him with a weak smile that quickly faded seeing how exhausted and ashen he looked. He approached the bed and sat down beside her, taking her hand in his.

"Ron, what are we doing here and why am I lying in this bed?" she asked with a hint of irritation.

"According to the doctor, you had an anxiety attack. Don't you remember getting short of breath and collapsing in our living room?"

Before Joy could answer, their minister appeared at the doorway. In that instant, everything came back to her. *My boy is dead! Dear Lord, no! No!* The grief that seized her reached to the depths of her soul. She was being pulled into a black pit; despair was all around her.

Her husband and the minister were now a blur and she could feel her chest begin to heave. A guttural sound was erupting within her, and it was beyond her control. Her wailing brought a nurse and emergency physician running into the room. Ron was holding her, rocking her. It was little consolation. She felt a stick in her upper left arm. The relief she so desperately needed was on its way.

****

Katelyn was enjoying the view from the cedar deck of Dan's two-storey North Vancouver home when she received the distressing call from Cheryl advising her that Adam's body had been found. Conversing until her friend was too overcome to continue, Katelyn set her cell phone down and sighed; a sickening feeling was beginning to form in the pit of her stomach. How had Adam's life turned so tragic? Her heart ached for the Wilson family.

Focusing on a bald eagle soaring majestically and effortlessly just above a grove of pine trees, Katelyn tried to make sense of the entire situation. She felt Dan's arms wrap around her waist and immediately took comfort in his embrace. "Bad news, Kate?"

Katelyn placed her hands on his and rested her head against his chest. "That call was from Cheryl. Adam's body was recovered from Lake Ontario. The police say he was murdered."

"Christ," Dan muttered.

"It appears Detective Wyatt was right. Adam became involved with the wrong people." She shook her head in disgust. "I used to adore that man, Dan. The genuine Adam Wilson was my first true love. He was sweet, sensitive and wouldn't intentionally hurt anyone. How on earth does someone like that turn to a life of crime?"

"That's one for the psychiatrists to answer, my love. I don't know."

Katelyn continued to watch the bald eagle, now joined by its mate, fly off into the distance, then change course and make its way back. "I could see a change in him, but never dreamed he would ever steal from people or get involved with criminals."

Dan held her tightly against him. "How would you know, Kate? Even his own family was unaware of the double life he led."

"They must be absolutely devastated. According to Cheryl, they had been clinging to the hope that he was somewhere in the Caribbean and would one day come home to face the allegations. It will be so hard for them to pick up the pieces and carry on."

Suddenly struck by a thought, she stepped away from his embrace and swung around to face him. Her eyes were wide with revelation. "Oh, my gosh!" she gasped. "Why didn't I think of it before?"

"Think of what?" Dan asked curiously.

"The Caribbean. Adam told me he travelled to the Cayman Islands twice a year." Katelyn picked up her iPhone and flipped through the directory until she found the number she was searching for.

"So? What about it?" Dan prodded.

"Wouldn't someone like Adam want to keep as much money out of the hands of the government as possible?" She held up her index finger for a moment before Dan could respond. Speaking into the phone, she said, "Detective Mike Wyatt please."

Dan's puzzled expression suddenly changed and a grin appeared on his face. "An offshore bank account in the Cayman Islands. You're brilliant!"

****

Wyatt had been through every document seized from Wilson's home and office and found nothing that indicated he held an offshore account. Of course, the paperwork could have been stashed elsewhere; out of sight from Revenue Canada had the government agency decided to audit him at some point. There was one other source of information Wyatt hadn't yet tapped into—Wilson's laptop computer. With the assistance of an officer from the Technological Crime Unit, he was able to access Wilson's emails and personal folders. Clicking on a folder entitled *Banking*, Wyatt scanned the long list of messages. The words *Grand Cayman* appeared in half a dozen subject lines. Placing the cursor on one such email, he double-clicked. As he read the message, his heart leapt in his chest. "Jackpot!" he said under his breath. He loved the feeling of euphoria that came from breaking a case, or stumbling onto evidence pertinent to an investigation. This was why he became a police officer. He continued to read every message in the *Banking* folder and when he finished reading the last email, the bank name, branch and Wilson's offshore account number had been revealed. But Wyatt's discovery was bittersweet. Investigations that carried into foreign countries were long and involved, and he knew the process could take months. Adding insult to injury, the Canadian government didn't have a treaty with the Cayman Islands, an agreement between the two countries to work together in preventing and prosecuting criminal activity, including money laundering and fraud cases. Had the offshore account been in the Bahamas or Jamaica where treaties with Canada existed, Wyatt would have been required to complete an MLAT—Mutual Legal Assistance Treaty application—formally asking the Bahamian or Jamaican authorities for assistance in the investigation of Wilson, and submit it through the Canadian Department of Justice. Without the treaty application, it would be more difficult to investigate Wilson's banking activity. The Cayman Islands had stricter privacy laws, and the Cayman authorities weren't obligated to cooperate. No doubt, Wilson would have known that at the time he opened the account.

Wyatt had his work cut out for him. He would begin by attempting to communicate directly with the Cayman Island Royal Police Service.

He would need a contact from their Financial Crime Unit who would be able to advise him of the police service's protocol and how to proceed with requesting assistance in the case. Pulling the chair closer to his cluttered desk and donning his reading glasses, he searched for a pen and pad of writing paper. Locating both under a stack of periodicals, Wyatt then opened the file labelled *Adam Wilson*. The first document visible was a newly obtained copy of a toxicological report from the coroner's office, indicating traces of benzoylmethylecgonine—cocaine—were discovered in Wilson's blood. Stapled behind it was a copy of the autopsy report. Flipping the documents over, Wyatt scanned the next several pages—complaints from four more investors: a retired couple from Vineland, a fifty-eight-year-old dentist from St. Catharines and a thirty-five-year-old businesswoman who, at one time, had been romantically involved with Wilson. He continued flipping until he arrived at the complaint made by Katelyn Ross near the back of the file. Her hunch was correct. He recalled the excitement in her voice as she described her Caribbean conversations with Wilson. She told Wyatt she wasn't anxious for restitution for herself, but for Wilson's other victims who were retired or near retirement. They needed the money now more than she did. Wyatt remembered thinking at the time that Margaret Ross would have been proud of her daughter.

## Chapter Twenty-One

It had been a month since the attack, and through physiotherapy and weight training, Dan regained full mobility in his arm and shoulder. The recurring nightmares had subsided allowing him to sleep through the entire night. His personal and professional lives were exactly where he wanted them to be; he was on a high and didn't ever want to come down. He wanted Katelyn near him constantly, and during the times he had to leave Vancouver on business, he hated every minute he was away from her.

Dan returned from spending most of the week in Victoria and was anxious to see Katelyn again. Arriving at her condominium and stepping off the elevator, a bottle of white wine in one hand and a dozen red roses in the other, she was there to greet him with a long and tender kiss.

"I've been waiting to do that all week," she said, breathless.

Dan's heart was pounding. "Lord, I've missed you, Kate," he replied, hugging her tightly.

"And I've missed you."

Breaking their embrace, he handed Katelyn the bouquet of flowers.

"Thank you, they're beautiful," she said before burying her nose into the soft, opened petals of one rose.

"Beside you, my love, they pale in comparison." Dan noticed she was wearing a tight pair of jeans, and a white tank top that showed off her midriff and accentuated her bustline. Her hair was tied back in a ponytail, making her look younger than her thirty years. He held her hand as they walked down the hall to her unit. Once inside, Dan stored the wine in the refrigerator while Katelyn placed the flowers in her mother's crystal vase.

"What message does red convey?" Katelyn asked. She knew the answer but wanted to hear the words.

"Dark red signifies my deep love for you," Dan replied as he came up behind her, slid his arms around her tiny waist and kissed her ear.

She turned to face him, melting in his embrace, his male hardness pressing against her body. "And I love you. You know, there's plenty of time before dinner, my Adonis," she said while unbuttoning his shirt.

Without saying a word, Dan took Katelyn's hands and placed them on his shoulders, then cupping his own hands under her buttocks, he lifted her up off the floor. She wrapped her legs around his waist and he quickly carried her to the bedroom. Dan sat down on the bed with Katelyn situated in his lap, their lips pressed together in a passionate kiss. She pushed the shirt over his broad shoulders and down his arms. She ran her hands over his chest, enjoying the feel of hard muscle under his soft skin. Dan's hands were on their own journey, travelling inside her t-shirt to stroke her back before bringing them around to caress her breasts. Pausing from the kiss to lift her arms, he pulled the garment up and over her head, letting the shirt fall to the floor. With both hands supporting Katelyn's back, Dan gently eased her body into a partially lateral position so her breasts pointed upward. His mouth descended over her bosom, and she welcomed his tongue with a soft groan as it traced circles over the entire area of one breast ending with her nipple, travelling down to tarry in the valley before making its way up to the expanse of her other breast. Katelyn could feel the cool trail of air on her skin as it met the warm wetness of Dan's tongue. Pulling her back into a sitting position, Dan then placed his hands on Katelyn's waist, lifted her out of his lap and laid her down onto the bed. He unbuttoned and unzipped her jeans, sliding them over her hips and down her legs to expose a pale pink thong. He ran his hand across the soft, cotton triangle before carefully removing it. As he kissed her pubic softness, Katelyn moaned at the sensation of his mouth and warm breath between her legs.

"You make me feel so incredibly good," she whispered. "My body is yearning for you to come inside me."

Dan stood up and quickly removed his remaining clothing, deeply aroused at the sight of Katelyn, her legs parted, revealing her womanly beauty and inviting him into her softness and warmth. Joining her on the bed, he gently took her in his arms. Lying on their sides, their bodies intertwined, Katelyn reached down and guided Dan's erection inside her, wet and waiting.

"Mercy, Kate," he groaned and began to slowly move his pelvis back and forth.

She gently massaged his buttocks and pushed his body tighter against hers, wanting to feel the entire length of his maleness.

Feeling the cool softness of her flesh meeting his, and the hardness of her nipples tickling his chest, he murmured in her ear, "You're body feels so good against mine. I love your softness and your scent."

After a short while, Katelyn repositioned herself on top of him. Dan not only enjoyed the sensation of her straddling him, he loved watching her as she moved her body provocatively and derived pleasure from her own touch. Knowing this, Katelyn looked at him and smiled seductively as she raised her arms above her head and removed the clip from her ponytail. She slowly let her hair fall around her shoulders, all the while rhythmically moving her hips back and forth and from side to side. She closed her eyes as her hands travelled down to her breasts and lightly moved in slow, circular motions over her skin before continuing their descent to her belly. She finished by arching her back and slowly bending backward, relishing the sensation of Dan's hardness rubbing against her pubic bone. Within seconds, the couple came together, crying out in sexual release, their bodies glistening with perspiration. As she lay in his arms, Katelyn felt an inner glow of contentment.

"That was one hell of an appetizer," Dan joked.

Katelyn giggled. "Just wait until dessert!"

****

"Seeing that you cooked such a delicious meal, the least I can do is clean up," Dan said as he rose from the dining room table and began stacking the dirty plates and flatware.

"Thank you for the compliment and for your offer. While you're doing that, I'll prepare the bedroom for the final course," replied Katelyn.

Balancing plates, empty water glasses and serving bowls containing remnants of a spinach salad and shrimp stir-fry with wild rice, Dan looked at her with amusement. "Then you weren't kidding about dessert?"

With a devilish grin, she replied, "I'll see you there in ten minutes."

Dan's curiosity was piqued, and after loading the dishwasher and tidying the kitchen, he made his way to the bedroom with anticipation. Opening the door, he found the room bathed in candlelight. Soft instrumental music was playing low. Looking around, his eyes focussed on Katelyn who was lighting the remaining pillar candle situated on the nightstand. She was dressed in a revealing white negligee that tied at the bodice with white satin ribbon. Her hair was styled on top of her head; soft tendrils surrounded her face and hung down her neck. Dan felt the familiar stirring in his groin and his pulse began to race.

"Welcome to Chez Kate, sir. May I show you to your seat?" Katelyn smiled seductively as she gestured to the bed. Dan could see the pillows had been plumped, and sheets neatly pulled back. Next to the bed was a side table displaying bowls filled with sauces of chocolate and butterscotch, maple syrup, and whipping cream.

Chuckling, he walked in her direction and replied, "Yes, please do!" The excitement was building inside him.

"Here, let me take your clothes." Katelyn slowly unbuttoned and removed Dan's shirt before moving her hands in circular motions along his chest and down to his waist. She knelt on the floor and unzipped Dan's jeans, pulling them over his hips and down to his feet. Her fingers momentarily and delicately acknowledged his arousal. Returning to a standing position, she took his hand and led him the remaining few steps to the bed. "Lie down and we'll begin."

Reclining on the bed, Dan looked up at Katelyn and noticed how angelic she looked in the candlelight. Her nakedness beneath the silky material was alluring, and he reached out to move his hand up and down her leg. It wasn't just her body that excited him. Yes, she was beautiful, but it was more than that. It had been many years since Dan experienced the kind of sexual chemistry he was now enjoying with Katelyn. Like many marriages, over time, he and his ex-wife became complacent. Their lovemaking had become routine with very little interest in change. Katelyn brought out a renewed excitement in Dan that had lain dormant inside him for a long time. Her adventuresome, uninhibited and very sensual spirit gave him a feeling of absolute exhilaration.

First dipping her finger in the bowl of maple syrup, Katelyn then applied it to his lips. Gingerly licking the sweet liquid from

Dan's mouth, she then plunged her tongue inside and kissed him passionately. Taking her face in his hands, Dan returned the kiss and sucked the maple flavour from her tongue. He could have spent half the night locked in that kiss, but moments later Katelyn pulled away, her attention again turning to the bowls of sweet sauces.

"Close your eyes," she whispered. "This will be a sensual experience I hope pleases you."

Dan did as he was told. Within seconds, he felt a tickling sensation on his left breast, then over to his right, then down his torso stopping at his navel. It was wet and had the aroma of butterscotch. Starting at his navel, she followed the trail of sauce with her tongue until she reached his pecs where she closed her mouth around each nipple and circled them with the tip of her tongue.

Dan lay totally relaxed and completely aroused, focussed solely on the sensation of Katelyn's tongue and lips on his skin.

Again, she softly planted her mouth upon his, her body stretched out on top of him. Dan could feel the hardness of her nipples through the soft, filmy fabric. He wrapped his arms around her and pressed her tightly to him.

Breaking away once more, she whispered, "Turn onto your stomach now," before sliding her body off his. Dan was more than happy to oblige and changed positions. He felt the tickle of liquid being drizzled over his shoulder blades and down to the small of his back. He closed his eyes, taking pleasure in the sensation of her tongue slowly following the path of sweetness. Dan felt Katelyn's hands underneath him, gently lifting his abdomen while a soft pillow was slid under his hips. A light substance he presumed to be whipped cream was then slathered over his raised buttocks. The mounting anticipation as he waited for the sensation of Katelyn's tongue to work its magic was a remarkable feeling, and when it travelled inside his crease to caress the hidden location within, Dan groaned, "My lord, Kate. That feels incredible."

"I'm so glad you're enjoying it," she said, removing the pillow and guiding him to the original position on his back.

To say he was thoroughly enjoying the decadent experience was an understatement. Eager to feel the next sensation she had planned for him, Dan felt Katelyn's fingers lightly encircle his throbbing erection, followed by a wetness that enveloped it. He could detect the sweet smell of chocolate. Knowing what was to follow, he hoped he could hang on long enough to take in the entire experience.

"For me, there's no better flavour than chocolate, and no better place to enjoy it than from this very spot," Katelyn whispered. Starting with the tip, she then moved her tongue up his shaft in long strokes.

Dan was inching closer and closer to release. When Katelyn enclosed her mouth around him and sucked the remaining chocolate away, he cried out, climaxing higher than he ever thought he could.

Katelyn waited for Dan's breathing to return to normal before situating her body on top of his, and resting her head on his chest.

Dan held her close and chuckled, "I must say, mademoiselle, the service you provided was impeccable. Chez Kate is five star!"

"Thank you, sir. I'm happy that you're happy," she replied. "Just don't forget my tip!"

****

"My goodness, I must be in heaven!" Katelyn whispered, experiencing the sweetness of orgasm as it flooded over her. She wished the glorious sensation wasn't so fleeting.

"I'm the one in heaven," Dan said with deep emotion, "because I'm making love with an angel."

Struck by the quiver in his voice and the beauty of his words, Katelyn opened her eyes and looked up into her lover's face. Dan was still inside her, but she knew these weren't the flippant words of a man on the verge of climaxing.

"I love you, Kate. With all my heart, I love you."

"And I love you." Overwhelmed, she began to cry. Pulling his face down to hers, she kissed him softly.

Whenever the couple came together, their lovemaking was slow, sweet and enduring. They communicated their desires during foreplay and intercourse; their exploration of each other was always leisurely, never hurried. The results were explosive and transcendent. Katelyn had never experienced such tenderness in a lover. Dan's touch was always gentle, his kisses feathery soft. Her pleasure was all that mattered to him and he never let her down. He always left her entirely satisfied and blissfully exhausted.

Still locked in the kiss, Dan began to move slowly and rhythmically inside her, and she moved her hips in time with his until he reached his sexual plateau. Katelyn loved the notion that the look and feel of her body could give her lover so much pleasure. Drowsy from their hours of lovemaking, Dan massaged Katelyn's back and whispered, "Sweet dreams, my angel." She closed her eyes and sighed, fully enjoying the sensation of his hands softly moving along her shoulders and down to the small of her back, where he traced the outline of her butterfly tattoo with his finger. It was the last thing she remembered until waking up in his arms the following morning.

## Chapter Twenty-Two

Joy Wilson was living in a black pit of emptiness, being tormented daily by thoughts of regret, guilt, anger and revenge, wanting only to be left alone. *Is this what hell is like?* She gazed out the window looking down at the yard below. The foliage on the shrubs and trees were changing colour; the daylight hours were receding. The songbirds had left on their migratory flight to warmer climates. The harshness of winter would soon be arriving. To Joy, it didn't matter. If she spent her remaining days holed up in this room, chain smoking cigarettes, that was fine by her. Actually, she welcomed the isolation. It had become too difficult to receive visitors, trying to make conversation and pretending to appear interested. Hell, she didn't even want to see her family at times. She hated not being able to support her husband and daughter. Their grief was just as real, just as deep.

She was tired of what the world had to offer: the cruelty, the pain, the ugliness. Her son was gone, his precious life snatched away by a piece of scum who had probably been raised by a piece of scum. No amount of tranquilizers or anti-depressants would change that fact. Her thoughts of Adam were obsessive and some days she cried herself to exhaustion. She refused to medicate, to go around feeling numb, suppressing her true self with pills.

Joy watched as Ron turned the dark soil in the perimeter garden in preparation for bulb planting. Spring seemed a lifetime away. She spied an overweight grey squirrel carrying a prized peanut in its mouth running the entire length of their wooden fence until it reached a neighbour's maple tree, choosing to settle in the lower branches. The rodent's bushy tail twitched in time to each loud throaty growl of warning it directed at an even more irritated blue jay jumping from branch to branch in a nearby pine tree. The commotion caused Ron to stop digging and focus his attention on the trees overhead. He leaned on his shovel, and Joy heard him address the bird by saying, "Did he steal your peanut or are you trying to steal his?" The jay let out one final squawk before flying away and out of view. As though Ron sensed she was watching, he turned his head in Joy's direction. Smiling, he shrugged his shoulders. Her face expressionless, Joy turned away from the window.

****

Wyatt arrived at the office an hour later than usual. A winter snowstorm had made roads treacherous, and morning rush hour traffic was a crawl. Throwing his wet winter jacket over a chair, his eyes fell on a large UPS package placed strategically on his desk. Looking at the shipping label, he noticed it was from the Royal Cayman Islands Police Service. Feeling like a child on Christmas morning, Wyatt excitedly ripped open the package. From previous conversations with the Cayman Islands police officers assisting him in the investigation, Wyatt knew what lay inside—copies of bank statements from a single account dating from when Wilson first opened it four years ago to the present time, and showing deposits and withdrawals made until shortly before he went missing. Wyatt quickly scanned the records, month by month, until he reached the most current statement. His eyes moved down to the bottom of the document, and there it was in black and white—a balance of $501,627.29.

****

Katelyn zigzagged along the smooth asphalt path on her rollerblades, careful not to collide with the cyclists who, like herself and Dan, were taking advantage of the unusually warm late-February temperatures. As she glided along the seawall lining the perimeter of Stanley Park, the ocean wind on her face and through her hair was refreshing. Dan was a few strides ahead of her. The mountain and ocean scenery weren't the only views she was taking in; she was enjoying the sway of Dan's hips as he stroked from side to side.

They had reached Prospect Point, the half-way mark of the ten kilometre trail, when the familiar ring of Katelyn's iPhone emanated from the pocket of her hoodie. "Dan, wait!" she called, stopping to answer the call.

Dan doubled back and slowly rolled to a stop in front of her.

She lifted the phone to her ear. "Katelyn Ross. Hello, Mike, how are you?"

Dan watched her as she listened intently to the voice at the other end of the line. The sun brought out streaks of shimmering bronze and ginger in her hair. Her sunglasses sat perched on the bridge of her freckled nose and concealed any hint of expression in her eyes; however, a broad smile had formed on her lips. She and the officer had become friends over the past year, and Dan was grateful to Wyatt for his assistance and support throughout the ordeal.

"I can't believe it! Mike, that is fantastic!" Katelyn was saying as she rotated in a circle on her rollerblades. "I'm so pleased. I'll contact my lawyer and give him the good news ... Hey, I just had a hunch—

thank you so much for looking into it. ... Yes, as a matter of fact we're outdoors enjoying the beautiful weather right now ... Br-r-r-r, that's cold! I don't miss those temperatures. Hopefully this weather system will head east and give you a nice February thaw." Katelyn laughed at Wyatt's response and ended the call by saying, "Okay, I'll talk to you soon. Keep warm!"

Pocketing her iPhone with one hand and taking Dan's hand with the other, she exclaimed, "Fantastic news, Adonis! The police were able to locate a bank account of Adam's in Grand Cayman, and just over half a million dollars were seized. Arrangements are being made to have the money transferred to Ontario and the courts will take it from there. We're in the home stretch!"

Dan shook his head in disbelief and whistled. "Five hundred thousand, eh? Chalk one up for the good guys. That's wonderful news, Angel." He pulled her to him and hugged her tightly, almost throwing them off balance. They laughed, trying to keep the other from falling.

Taking off her sunglasses, she looked deep into his eyes. "Now I can put this ugly part of my past behind me and concentrate on our future together. I love you, and I am so blessed to have you in my life."

"And I love you," Dan replied. He kissed her tenderly, and for a few moments there was no one in the world except the two of them.

The couple continued on their journey, skating hand in hand until a group of cyclists split them up and they were forced once again to skate in tandem. Katelyn felt a renewed sense of spirit. It was one month shy of a year since her mother died, and throughout the weeks and months that had followed, her grief had gradually diminished.

Similar to that grief, the anger and betrayal she suffered at the hands of Adam Wilson would also fade away with time.

****

The load on Ron's shoulders was a little lighter this particular winter morning as he pulled his decade-old, gray Chevy Blazer into the snow-covered driveway of the Wilson home. Returning from an appointment with his lawyer, he was pleased to hear the victims would receive partial restitution, and the civil litigation against Adam's estate was in its final stages. The family had been allowed to lay claim to a few personal belongings before the remainder of Adam's property was auctioned off by court order, the proceeds turned over to the plaintiffs in the case. It had been a long road for everyone involved. The investigation into Adam's murder was ongoing, and although there were no new leads, Detective Haines had assured Ron the homicide detectives were busy following up on the information already provided to them.

He unlocked the back door and entered the kitchen. As usual, the house was quiet. Abby had found an apartment closer to her workplace and moved out with her cat the first weekend in January. Ron would have preferred she postpone the relocation indefinitely; he enjoyed having her home, but he knew she needed to be in an emotionally healthier environment. The fallout from Adam's death, and the events leading up to its confirmation, had taken a toll on the Wilson family.

Ron was now living a solitary lifestyle. He cooked the meals, cleaned the house, washed the clothes and shopped, all the chores Joy had insisted on doing before their son's disappearance. It was no trouble. He missed his wife. The active, enthusiastic and outspoken woman he knew all these years was gone. He prayed it was only temporary. He had tried to get her to see a therapist, but she flatly refused. She was now distant and said very little, not wishing to see anyone. He could not even get her to venture out to the garden. When she wasn't sleeping, she was sitting at the bedroom window, her eyes unfocussed. She preferred smoking to eating, and Ron guessed her weight was now below one hundred pounds. She hadn't been that thin since high school. Any show of concern on his part pertaining to Joy's health resulted in either an angry outburst or cold silence from her. He slept in the guest bedroom when he wasn't falling asleep in his recliner. He was now spending most of his free time in front of the fifty-two inch flat screen television Adam had given them for a Christmas gift two years ago. It was a diversion from all of the madness. At times, he couldn't help but wonder if his son had purchased the T.V. with illegally obtained money.

Ron retrieved a beer from the fridge, popped the tab and took a long swig. It would be one of many he planned on putting back before the day was over. Even though he had checked on his wife before leaving for the appointment almost two and a half hours ago, and found her sleeping soundly, he decided to look in on her again. Maybe she was awake and would feel like talking today, or come down to the kitchen for a bowl of soup or cup of tea. All he could do was hope.

Opening the door to the master bedroom, he was taken aback by the rancid smell of vomit mixed with the odour of stale cigarette smoke. His eyes scanned the entire room, his brain taking snapshot after snapshot of the scene that appeared before him. His wife's frail body, dressed in a pale blue flannel nightgown, lay supine across the bed. An empty twenty-four ounce bottle of vodka had tipped over, the remaining contents spilled out, forming a small puddle on the hardwood floor. An empty prescription pill bottle sat teetering on the edge of the nightstand.

Finally comprehending what had taken place, Ron ran over to the bed. Horrified, he screamed, "Joy!" No response. "Joy!" He touched her wrist; her skin was cool. He couldn't feel her pulse. Ron placed his fingers on the side of her neck—nothing. Her face was ashen and her eyes were partially open. Dried vomit encrusted her lips and had travelled from the corners of her mouth, down her neck, pooling on the sheet and into her unkempt hair.

"Dear God, please don't take her from me!" he cried, grabbing the receiver of the bedside telephone and dialling 911. Waiting for the operator, he spied a note in Joy's handwriting lying next to the phone. He picked it up and as he read it, he began to weep.

# *Epilogue*

Dan rose up from the turquoise blue expanse of the Pacific Ocean, droplets of seawater glistening on his golden chest and shoulders. As he approached the two lounging chairs, Katelyn looked up from her novel, taking in every detail of the half-naked, irresistibly sexy man in front of her. She reached out her hand and he took it, kissing her palm.

"I could sure get used to this life," he said, wrapping a towel around his waist. "I wonder what the chef's got on the dinner menu tonight."

Katelyn laughed. "I hope you won't be too disappointed once we get back to regular everyday living. I may have to take some gourmet cooking classes!"

Dan nodded, trying to keep from smiling. "Ya, judging by the taste of your coq au vin, the classes are a good idea!"

Katelyn gasped, pretending to be hurt, and slapping him on the buttocks with her book.

Laughing, he bent down over her and said, "I'm kidding, Angel." He kissed her. "Why don't we take a nap before dinner?"

She could tell by his impish grin that sleep wasn't what he had in mind.

"What a tantalizing idea! Lead the way!" Rising from the chaise, Katelyn gathered up her beach bag, towel and sandals.

Holding hands, the couple made their way up the short sandy path, through the lush, fragrant gardens to the rear entrance of the sprawling two-storey mansion owned by John Carrington. A limousine and driver, housekeeper, personal chef and masseuse were at the couple's disposal during their two week stay in Kauai. It was John's wedding gift to Katelyn and Dan.

# About the Author

Kathryn Jesson resides in the Greater Toronto area with her husband, Mike, and their Miniature Pinscher/Jack Russell Terrier, Missy.